"THAT'S MY DAD!"

Bolivar said, walking around the thing and admiring it from all angles.

It looked roughly like a miniature tyrannosaurus rex with advanced leprosy and molting fur. A biped for the obvious reason that I was one. The heavy tail, that bifurcated into sucker-tipped tentacles at the end, both balanced the weighty device and contained storage space for the power plant and equipment. An oversized jaw, just aswarm with yellow and green teeth, adorned the front of the head; a little buck-toothed, too, like its maker. Ears like a bat, whiskers like a rat, eyes like a cat, gills like a spratt—it really was loathsome. The front split open and I climbed carefully inside . . .

Bantam Science Fiction
Ask your bookseller for the books you have missed

FANTASTIC VOYAGE by Isaac Asimov
MONUMENT by Lloyd Biggle, Jr.
ROGUE IN SPACE by Fredric Brown
WHAT MAD UNIVERSE by Fredric Brown
BEASTS by John Crowley
DHALGREN by Samuel R. Delany
NOVA by Samuel R. Delany
TRITON by Samuel R. Delany
UBIK by Philip K. Dick
NEBULA WINNERS TWELVE edited by Gordon Dickson
TIME STORM by Gordon Dickson
ALAS, BABYLON by Pat Frank
THE STAINLESS STEEL RAT WANTS YOU!
    by Harry Harrison
HELLSTROM'S HIVE by Frank Herbert
DEMON SEED by Dean Koontz
NEBULA AWARD STORIES ELEVEN edited by
    Ursula K. LeGuin
THE DAY OF THE DRONES by A. M. Lightner
DRAGONSONG by Anne McCaffrey
DRAGONSINGER by Anne McCaffrey
A CANTICLE FOR LEIBOWITZ by Walter M. Miller, Jr.
HIGH COUCH OF SILISTRA by Janet E. Morris
THE GOLDEN SWORD by Janet E. Morris
WIND FROM THE ABYSS by Janet E. Morris
LOGAN'S RUN by William F. Nolan &
    George Clayton Johnson
LOGAN'S WORLD by William F. Nolan
MAN PLUS by Frederik Pohl
CRITICAL MASS by Frederik Pohl & C. M. Kornbluth
THE FEMALE MAN by Johanna Russ
THE JONAH KIT by Ian Watson
NEBULA AWARD STORIES NINE edited by Kate Wilhelm

THE
STAINLESS STEEL RAT
WANTS YOU!

HARRY HARRISON

THE STAINLESS STEEL RAT WANTS YOU!

A Bantam Book / August 1979
2nd printing .... October 1979
3rd printing .... March 1981

All rights reserved.
Copyright © 1979 by Harry Harrison.
Cover art copyright © 1979 by Bantam Books, Inc.
This book may not be reproduced in whole or in part, by
mimeograph or any other means, without permission.
For information address: Bantam Books, Inc.

ISBN 0–553–20016–X

Published simultaneously in the United States and Canada

Bantam Books are published by Bantam Books, Inc. Its trade-
mark, consisting of the words "Bantam Books" and the por-
trayal of a bantam, is Registered in U.S. Patent and Trademark
Office and in other countries. Marca Registrada. Bantam
Books, Inc., 666 Fifth Avenue, New York, New York 10103.

PRINTED IN THE UNITED STATES OF AMERICA

14 13 12 11 10 9 8 7 6 5 4 3

ONE

Blodgett is a peaceful planet. The sun shines orangely, gentle breezes cool the brow, while the silent air is disturbed only slightly by the distant rumble of rockets from the spaceport. Very relaxing—but too much so for one like myself who must stay on guard, alert and aware at all times. And I admit that I was doing none of these things when the front door announcer bing-bonged. Hot water splattered my head and I was drowsy as a comatose cat.

"I'll get that," Angelina called out, loud enough to be heard over the splash of the shower. I gurgled an answer as I reluctantly turned the thing off and climbed out.

The drier blanketed me with warm air while the lotion mist tickled my nose. I hummed to myself with sybaritic joy, at peace with the world, naked as the day I was born—except of course for the few devices that I am never without. Voluntarily, that is. Life had its joys and, as I appreciated my stalwart body and rugged face in the mirror—the touch of gray at the temples *did* add a distinguished note—I could think of nothing to worry about.

Other than the sudden angst that gripped me, chilling me to the bone. Was this a psi premonition? No, it was the ticking away of seconds. Angelina had been far too long at the door. Something was wrong.

I burst out into the hall and down it at a run. The house was empty. Then I was through the front door and bounding down the path like a pink gazelle, hopping desperately on one leg as I wrenched the pistol from my ankle holster, my eyes bulging in shock at the sight of my Angelina being bustled into a black ground car by two burly types. It pulled away and I risked a single shot at its tires, but could not fire again because there was traffic beyond.

Angelina! I ground my teeth with rage, fired more

1

shots into the air so that the spectators who had been admiring my nude form now dived for cover. I managed to keep just enough peace of mind to memorize the numbers on the car.

Back in the house I thought briefly of calling the police, as any good citizen would, but since I have always been a very bad citizen I instantly dismissed the idea. Mighty is Slippery Jim diGriz in his wrath. Revenge would be mine. I turned on the compterm, mashed my thumbprint onto the ID plate, punched in my priority code, then the number of the kidnap car and asked for identification. Not a very complex task for a planetary computer and the answer appeared on the screen as soon as I hit the PRINT button.

When it did I dropped numbly into the chair. *They* had her.

This was far worse than I had imagined. Now, look, don't go thinking that I am a coward. Quite the opposite, I say humbly. You are looking at a survivor of a lifetime of crime—who has also survived another lifetime of crime-fighting after being drafted into the Special Corps, the elite galaxy-wide organization that uses crooks to catch crooks. That I have stayed relatively sound in wind and body all these years certainly speaks well of my reflexes, if not my intelligence. It was now going to take all my years of experience to extract my dear wife from this nasty situation. Thought was needed, not action and, though it was still early in the day, I cracked out a bottle of 140 proof Old Thought Provoker and poured a generous amount to lubricate my synapses.

With the first sip came the realization that the boys would have to be in on this one. Angelina and I, doting parents, had labored to shield them from the cruel facts of the world, but that time was over. Their graduation from school was still a few days away, but I was sure that this could be accelerated with the correct persuasion in the proper quarters. Strange to think they were almost out of their teens already; how the years slip by. Their mother—*Angelina, my kidnapped treasure!*—was as beautiful as ever. As for myself, I may be older but I am no wiser. The gray in my hair has not affected the lust for gold in my heart.

I did not waste a moment as I mumbled to myself nostalgically. Throwing on my clothes, kicking on my boots, stowing away about my person a number of lethal and technological devices, I dropped into the garage even as I closed the last closure. My bright red Firebom 8000 exploded into the drive as the door snapped open and hurtled down the road, scattering the dull citizens of the peaceful planet of Blodgett in all directions. The only reason we had settled on this bucolic world was to be near the boys while they were at school. I would be delighted to leave the place without a backward glance. Not only had it all the boredom of an agricultural planet, it was also infested by an octopuslike bureaucracy. Since it was centrally located among a number of star systems, and boasted a salubrious climate, the bureaucrats and League administrators had moved in to create a secondary economy of government offices. I preferred the farmers.

The farms gave way to trees as I burned down the road, then to the barren rock hills. There was a chill in the air at this altitude that went with the somber stone cliffs and, when I whisked around the final turn, the damp morning perfectly matched the rough finish of the high stone wall ahead. As the spiked portcullis rumbled slowly upward I admired, not for the first time, the letters hacked into the black slab of steel by the entrance.

DORSKY MILITARY BOARDING SCHOOL AND PENITENTIARY

That my dear twins had to be incarcerated here! As a father I felt concern; as a citizen I suppose it was a blessing. What I thought was just good spirits in the lads, the rest of the world tended to frown upon. Before coming here they had been expelled from a total of 214 schools. Three of these schools had burned down under mysterious circumstances; another had blown up. I had never believed that the mass suicide attempt of all the senior masters at another school had anything to do with my boys; but vicious tongues will wag. In any case they had finally met their match, if not their master in old Colonel Dorsky. After being forcefully retired from the military he had opened the school and put his years of service, experience and sadism to work. My boys had reluctantly gained an education, served their term and in a few days would face the graduating ceremonies and parole. Only now things would have to be accelerated just a little bit.

As always I reluctantly surrendered my weapons, was X-rayed and spy-beamed, locked through the multiple automatic doors and released into the inner quad. Dispirited figures shuffled by, beaten down by the school's foolproof and escapeproof system. But there ahead, crossing the ferroconcrete artificial grass, were two upright and brisk figures, unbent by any despair. I whistled shrilly and they dropped their books and ran up to greet me warmly. After which I rose slowly to my feet and dusted myself off—then proved that an old dog can still teach the pups a trick or two. They laughed as they rubbed their sore spots and stood up again. They were a bit shorter than I was, taking after their mother there, but soundly muscled and handsome as gods. Many a girl's father would be out buying a shotgun after they were released from school.

"What was that bit with the arm and elbow, Dad?" James asked.

"Explanations can wait. I am here to accelerate your graduation because something not too nice has happened to your mother."

Their grins vanished on the instant and they leaned forward alertly, drinking in every word as I explained what I had seen, nodding in agreement.

"Right, then," Bolivar said. "We go stir up old Dirty Dorsky and get out of here . . ."

". . . and do something about it," James added, finishing the sentence. They did this often, many times thinking as one.

We marched. In step, at a good doubletime of 120 paces to the minute. Through the great hall and past all the skeletons in chains, up the main staircase, splashing through the water running constantly down it, and into the Head's office.

"You can't go in there," his secretary-bodyguard said, surging to his feet, 200 kilos of trained fighting flesh. We scarcely slowed and only broke step going over his unconscious body. Dorsky looked up growling when we came through the door, gun ready in his fist.

"Put it away," I told him. "It is an emergency and I have come for my sons a few days early. Would you be so kind as to give them their graduation certificates and expiration of term-served papers."

"Go to hell. No exceptions. Get out of here," he suggested.

I smiled at the unswerving gun and decided that explanation would be more fruitful than violence.

"This is a bit of an emergency. My wife, the boys' mother, was arrested this morning and taken away."

"It was due to happen. You lead undisciplined lives. Now get out."

"Listen, you dough-faced, moron-brained, military dinosaur, I came here for neither your sympathy nor malice. If this was an ordinary arrest the arrestees would have been unconscious soon after opening the door. Detectives, cops, military police, customs agents, none of those could stand before the wrath of my sweet Angelina."

"Well?" he said, puzzled, but gun barrel still ready.

"She went along quietly in order to give me time. Time that I will need. Because I checked the license plate numbers and these thugs were agents for . . ." I took a deep breath, ". . . agents for Interstellar Internal and External Revenue."

"The income tax men," he breathed and his eyes glowed redly. The gun vanished. "James diGriz, Bolivar diGriz, step forward. Accept these graduation certificates as token of your reluctant completion of all courses and of time served here. You are now alumni of Dorsky Military Boarding School and Penitentiary and I hope you will, like the other graduates, remember us with a little curse before retiring each night. I would shake your hands except my bones are getting brittle and I am laying off the hand-to-hand combat.

Go forth with your father and join him in the battle against evil and strike a blow for me as well."

That was all there was to it. A minute later we were out in the sunshine and climbing into the car. The boys left their childish possessions behind them in the school and entered the world of adult responsibility.

"They won't hurt Mom, will they?" James asked.

"They won't live long if they do," Bolivar said, and I distinctly heard his teeth grinding together.

"No, of course not. Getting her release will be easy enough, as long as we can get to the records in time."

"What records?" Bolivar asked. "And why did Dirty Dorsky help so easily? That's not like him."

"It *is* like him because under that veneer of stupidity, violence and military sadism he is still roughly human like the rest of us. And like us, he regards the tax man as the natural enemy."

"I don't understand," James said, then grabbed the handhold as we snarled around a tight bend just a micrometer from the edge of the vertical drop.

"Unhappily you will," I told him. "Your lives have been sheltered up until now, in that you have been spending but not earning. Soon you will be earning like the rest of us and, with the arrival of your first credit, sweat of your palms and brow, the tax man will arrive as well. Swooping in ever smaller circles, screaming shrilly, until he perches on your shoulder and with yellow beak bites most of the money from your grasp."

"You sure turn a nice simile, Dad."

"It's true, it's true," I muttered, swinging into the motorway and roaring into the fast lane. "Big government means big bureaucracy which means big taxes; there seems to be no way out of it. Once you're involved in the system you are trapped, and you end by paying more and more taxes. Your mother and I have a little nest egg put aside for investing for your future. Money earned before you lads were born."

"Money stolen before we were born," Bolivar said. "Profits from illegal operations on a dozen worlds."

"We didn't!"

"You did, Dad," James said. "We broke into enough

files and records to find out just where all the money came from."

"Those days are behind us!"

"We hope not!" both boys said in unison. "What would the galaxy be like without a few stainless steel rats to stir them up. We have heard your bedtime lectures about how bank robbery helps the economy. It gives the bored police something to do, the newspapers something to print, the population something to read about, the insurers something to pay off. It is a boost to the economy and keeps the money in circulation. It is the work of a philanthropist."

"No! I did not raise my boys to be crooks."

"You didn't?"

"Well, maybe to be *good* crooks. To take only from those who can afford it, to injure no one, to be kind, courteous, friendly and irreverent. To be crooked just long enough to be enlisted in the Special Corps where you can serve mankind best by tracking down the real crooks."

"And the real crooks we are tracking down now?"

"The income tax people! As long as your mother and I were stealing money and spending it there were no problems. But as soon as we took our hard-earned salaries in the Corps and invested them we ran afoul of the tax people. We made a few minor bookkeeping errors . . ."

"Like not reporting any of your profits?" James asked innocently.

"Yes, that's the sort of thing. By hindsight it was rather foolish. We should have gone back to robbing banks. So now we are enmeshed in their coils, playing their games, getting involved in court actions, audits, lawyers, fines, jail terms—the whole mess. There is only one answer, one final solution. That is why your mother went away calmly with these financial vampires. To leave me free to cut the Gordian knot and get us out of this mess."

"What will we have to do?" they asked in eager unison.

"Destroy all of our tax records in their files, that's what. And end up broke—but free and happy."

TWO

We sat in the darkened car and I nibbled nervously at my fingernails. "It's no good," I said at last. "I am racked with guilt. I cannot steer two innocents into a life of crime."

There were snorts, indicating strong emotions of some kind, from the back seat. Then the doors were hurled open and slammed shut again just as quickly and I looked up in shocked surprise as they both stamped away down the night-filled street. Had I driven them away? Would they attempt to do the job on their own and bungle it? What disasters lay ahead? I was fumbling with the door handle, trying to make my mind up, when the footsteps grew louder again, returning. I stepped out to meet them when they came back, faces grim and empty of humor.

"My name is James," James said, "and this is my brother, Bolivar. We are adults under law having passed the age of eighteen. We can legally drink, smoke, curse and chase girls. We can also, if we choose, decide to break any law or laws of any planet knowing full well that if we are caught in crime we will have to pay the penalty. We have heard a rumor from a relative that you, crooked Slippery Jim, are about to break the law in a singularly good cause and we want to sign up for the job. What do you say, Dad?"

What could I say? Was that a lump in the old rat's throat, a tear forming in his rodent eye? I hoped not; emotion and crime do not mix.

"Right," I snapped, in my best imitation of a drill sergeant with piles. "You're enlisted. Follow instructions, ask questions only if the instructions are unclear, otherwise do what I do, do what I say. Agreed?"

"Agreed!" they chorused.

"Then put these items into your pockets. They are bits of equipment which are sure to come in handy. Are you wearing your fingerprint gloves?" They raised their hands which glistened slightly in the streetlamp light. "Good. You will be happy to hear that you will be leaving the prints of the mayor of this city, as well as those of the chief of police. That should add a note of interest to an otherwise confusing situation. Now, do you know where we are going? Of course not. It's a large building around the corner which you cannot see from here. The area HQ of the IIER, Interstellar Internal and External Revenue. In there are records of all their larcenous endeavors . . ."

"You mean *yours,* don't you, Dad?"

"Larceny is in the eye of the beholder, my sons. They take a dim view of my activities, while I in turn look with loathing on their taking ways. Tonight we attempt to even the score. We do not approach the IIER building directly because it has many defenses since they know they are unloved. Instead we enter the building around this corner which, not by chance have I selected it, has a rear that adjoins our target building."

We walked while I talked and both boys recoiled a bit at the lights and crowds ahead. Sirens screamed as official black groundcars drew up, television cameras churned away, searchlights fanned across the sky. I smiled at their hesitation and patted their back as we walked.

"Now isn't that a lovely diversion? Who would consider breaking and entering in a setting like this? The opening night, the premier performance of the new opera *Cohoneighs in the Fire."*

"But we'll need tickets . . ."

"Bought from a scalper this afternoon at outrageous prices. Here we go."

We pushed through the crowd, surrendered our tickets, then made our way from here, not that I had any intention of listening to the bucolic mooing and lowing in any case. There were other advantages to the top of the building. We went to the bar first and I had a refreshing beer and was cheered to see that the lads ordered only nonalcoholic drinks. I was not so elated at other of their activities. Leaning close to Bolivar I took his arm lightly—then clamped down a tight index finger on the nerve that paralyzed his hand.

"Exceedingly naughty," I said as the diamond brace-let fell to the carpet from his numb fingers. I tapped an exceedingly porcine woman on the shoulder and pointed it out when she turned. "I beg your pardon, madam. But did that bracelet slip from your wrist? It did? No, let me. No, my pleasure indeed, thank you, and may he bless you as well for all eternity." I then turned about and slipped a steely gaze into James's ribs. He raised his hands in the sign of peace.

"I get the message, Dad. Sorry. Just keeping in practice. For extra practice I put the wallet back in the gent's pocket as soon as I saw Bolivar rubbing his numb arm."

"That's fine. But no more. We are on a serious mission tonight and want no petty crime to jeopardize our position. There, that's the last buzzer. Down drinks and away we go."

"To our seats?"

"Definitely not. To the gents."

We each occupied a cubicle, standing on the seats so our legs would not reveal our occupation of the prem-ises, and waited until all the footsteps had retreated and the last receptacle had been flushed. We waited even longer until the first waiting notes of the opera assault-ed our ears. The rush of running water had been far more musical.

"Here we go," I said, and we did.

A wet eye on the end of a damp tendril watched them leave. The tendril projected from the waste basket. The tendril was attached to a body that belonged in the wastebasket—or even more loath-some surroundings. It was bumpy, gnarled, ugly, clawed. Not nice.

"You seem to know your way around here pretty well," Bolivar said as we went through a locked door marked "Private," and along a dank corridor.

"When I bought the tickets this afternoon I let my-self in and ran a quick survey. Here we are."

I let the lads disconnect the burglar alarms them-selves, good practice, and was chuffed to see that they needed no instruction. They even put a few drops of friction-freer in the tracks before slipping the window silently open. We gazed out into the night at the dark form of a building a good five meters away.

"Is that it?" Bolivar asked.

"If it is—how do we get there?" James said.

"It is—and this is how." I slipped the gunlike object from my inside pocket and held it up by the looped and heavy handle. "It has no name since I designed and made it myself. When the trigger is pulled this projectile—shaped like a tiny plumber's friend—is hurled forth with great velocity. It trails behind a thin strand of almost unbreakable monomolecular filament. What happens then, you might ask, and I will be happy to tell. The shock of firing switches on a massive-charge battery in the projectile that expends all of its power in fifteen seconds. But during that time a magnetic field is created here on the projectile's tip that has enough gauss to hold up a thousand-kilo load. Simple, isn't it?"

"Are you sure *you're* not simple, Dad?" Bolivar asked, worried. "How can you be sure of hitting a piece of steel in the dark with that thing?"

"For two reasons, oh scoffing son. I discovered earlier today that each story of that building has a steel cornice over a steel beam. Secondly, with a magnetic field that strong it is hard to keep this thing away from any steel or iron. It turns as it goes and seeks its own nesting place. James, you have the climbing line? Good. Fasten one end to that sturdy-looking pipe, securely mind you since it is a long drop. That's it, let me have the other end. You are both now wearing your gloves with the armored palms? Capital. It will do your muscles good to swing across this bottomless chasm. I'll secure the line and twitch it three times when it is ready for you to cross. Here we go." I raised the vital piece of gadgetry.

"Good luck," they said as one.

"Thank you. The sentiment is appreciated, but not the idea. Stainless steel rats in the concrete wainscotting of society must make their own luck."

Cheered by my own philosophy I pulled the trigger. The projectile zinged away and found a nesting place with an audible splat. I pressed the button that drew the monofilament tight—then dived headlong through the open window. Fifteen seconds is not a long time. I bent and extended my legs and started to spin and cursed and hit all at the same moment. All of the impact came on one leg and, if it were not broken, it certainly wasn't feeling too good. This had not happened during the times I had practiced this maneuver at home. And the seconds were clicking away quite fast while I hung there numbly and swung about.

The nonfunctioning leg had to be ignored, hurt as it did. I tapped with my good leg and found the top of the window frame off to the left. I kicked out so I swung in that direction, letting out some line at the same time. This swung me out and brought me back in line with the window—which I hit with my good foot with all my weight behind it.

Nothing happened, of course, since window glass is pretty tough stuff these days. But my foot found the windowsill and struggled for a purchase as my scrabbling fingers sought a grip on the frame. At which precise instant the magnetic field released and I was on my own.

It was a sticky moment. I was holding myself in place by three fingertips and one insecurely planted toe-tip. My other leg dangled limply like an old salami. Below me was a black drop to sure death.

"Doing all right, Dad?" one of the boys whispered from behind me.

I must say it took a certain amount of internal discipline to control the rush of answers that surged to my lips; boys should not hear that sort of language from a parent. With an effort I contained the words and strangled out something that sounded like *fizzlesloop* while I fought for balance. I succeeded, though my fingers were growing tired already. With careful patience I clipped the now-defunct gadget to my waist and wriggled my fingers into the pocket that held the glasscutter.

This was no time for subtlety or sloth. Normally I would have applied the suction cup, cut out a small section of glass, lifted it free, opened the latch, etc. Not now. One quick whip of my arm delineated a rough circle and, in a continuation of the same motion, I made a fist and punched the circle hard. It fell into the room, I hurled the glasscutter after it—and reached in and grabbed the frame.

The glass hit the floor with a loud clang just as my toes slipped off the sill. I hung, dangling from one hand, trying to ignore the sharp edge of glass cutting into my arm. Then, ever so slowly, I bent my arm in a one-armed pullup—oh advantage of constant exercise —until I could reach in with my other hand for a more secure grip.

After this it was a piece of cake, though the blood on my arm tended to interfere with arrangements. Getting my foot back on the windowsill, unlocking and opening the window—after disconnecting the burglar alarm —sliding through to drop, quite limply, onto the floor.

"I think I'm getting a little old for this sort of thing," I muttered darkly to myself once my breath had returned. All was silent. The falling of the glass, loud though it had been to me, had apparently gone unheard in the empty building. To work. There was only silence now from the boys—that was professional, but I knew they would be worried. With my pinlight I found a secure anchor for the line, tied it and drew it tight, then twanged it soundly three times.

They were across in seconds.

"You had us worried," one of them understated.

"I had *me* worried! One of you take this light and a medpak and see if you can do something about this cut on my arm. Blood is evidence as you well know."

The slashes were superficial and soon bandaged; my numb leg hurt a good deal but was coming to life. I dragged it around in circles until some function was restored.

"That's it," I finally announced. "Now for the fun part."

I led the way out of the room and down the dark corridor, walking fast in an attempt to get normal operation back into the leg. The boys fell a bit behind so that I was a good three meters ahead of them when I turned the corner. So they were still concealed when the amplified voice roared out.

"Stay where you are, diGriz. You are under arrest!"

THREE

Life is full of little moments like this—or at least *my* life is. I can hardly speak for anyone else. They can be disconcerting, annoying, even deadly if one is not prepared for them. Happily, due to a certain amount of foresight and specialized knowledge, I was prepared for this one. The blackout-gas grenade in my hand was flying forward while the voice was still yammering away. It exploded with a flat boom, the black cloud poured out and many people complained angrily. To give them something else to complain about I flipped a gunfight simulator into the smoke. This handy device bangs and booms away like a small war, while at the same time ejecting pellets of laughing gas concentrate in all directions. Sowing a certain amount of confusion I must add. I turned quietly back to the boys who were frozen in midstride, eyes as wide and staring as poached eggs. I put finger to lip and waved them back down the corridor out of earshot of the simulated battle.

"Here is where we part," I said. "And here are the computer programming codes."

Bolivar took them by reflex, then shook his head as though to clear fuzz from his brain. "Dad, would you tell us . . ."

"Of course. When I had to punch the window out I knew that the sound, as small as it was, would be picked up by the security alarms. Therefore I switched to plan B, neglecting to tell you about it in case you might protest. Plan B involves my making a diversion while you two get down to the computer room and finish this job. Using my Special Corps priorities I managed to get all the details you will need to get access to the IIER memory files and to wipe them clean. A simple instruction to the brainless computer will destroy the files of all the individuals for light years around who are lucky enough to have their last names begin with the letter D. I see myself, at times, as a . . ."

"Dad!"

"I know, I'm sorry, I digress and ramble. After doing that you will also wipe the U and P files, in case they see some connection between my presence here and the destruction of the records. The selection of these other two letters is not by chance . . ."

"Since *dup* is the most insulting word in Blodgett slang."

"Right you are, James, your brain cells are really ticking over tonight. Your task complete, you will be able to exit from the ground floor by way of one of the windows and mingle with the crowd without being apprehended. Now isn't that a simple plan?"

"Except for the fact you get arrested it's a grand one," Bolivar said. "We can't let you do it, Dad."

"You can't stop me—but the sentiment is appreciated. Be sensible, lads. Blood is much easier to identify than fingerprints, and they have plenty of mine to play with back in that room. So if I escape now I am a fugitive on the run as soon as they make the analysis —beside the fact that they have already seen me. In any case, your mother is in prison and I do miss her and look forward to joining her there. With the tax records destroyed all they can hold me on is breaking and entering and I can post bail and jump it and we will all leave this planet forever."

"They may not allow bail," James worried.

"In that case your parents will easily crack out of the local crib. Not to worry. Go to your task and I'll off to mine. Return home afterward and get some sleep and I'll be in touch. Begone."

And, being sensible boys, they went. I returned to battle, pulling on goggles and inserting nose plugs. I had plenty of grenades—smoke, blackout, lachrymose, regurgitant—the IIER had made me throw up often enough and I wanted to return the favor—which

I strewed about with great liberality. Someone began firing a gun, pretty stupid considering that he had a better chance of shooting his own people than of winging me. I waded into the smoke, found him, rendered him unconscious with sharp blow that would give him a good-sized headache as well, then took the gun away. It had a full clip of bullets which I emptied into the ceiling.

"You'll never catch Slippery Jim!" I shouted into the noisy darkness, then led my pack of pecuniary pirates on a merry chase through the large building. I estimated how long it would take the boys to finish the job, added fifteen minutes as a safety precaution, then gratefully dropped onto a couch in the director's office, lit one of his cigars and relaxed.

"I surrender, I surrender," I shouted out to my stumbling, crying, puking pursuers, "you are too smart for me. Just promise that you won't torture me."

They crept in cautiously, their ranks swollen by the local police who had come to see what all the fun was about, as well as by a squad of combat troops in full battle gear. "All this for little me," I said, blowing a smoke ring in their direction. "I feel flattered. And I want to make a statement to the press about how I was kidnapped, brought here unconscious, then frightened and pursued. I want my lawyer."

Indeed they lacked any sense of humor and I was the only one smiling when I was led away. There was not too much rough stuff, too many people around for that, as well as the fact that it really went against the Blodgett personality. The best selling chewing gum on the planet was called Cud, and they really chewed it. Sirens screamed, cars raced and I was hauled off in irons.

Though not to prison, that was the funny part. We did reach the prison gate but were stopped at the entrance where there was a lot of shouting and even some fist waving. Then back into the cars and off again to the town hall where, to my surprise, the manacles were removed before I was led into the building. I knew something strange was happening when I was pushed through an unmarked door—with at least one boot toe helping me on my way. The door closed, I brushed my rumpled clothes, then turned and raised my eyebrows at the familiar figure in the chair behind the desk.

"What a pleasant surprise," I said. "Been keeping well . . . ?"

"I ought to have you shot, diGriz," he snarled.

Inskipp, my boss, head of the Special Corps, probably the man with the single greatest amount of power in the galaxy. The Special Corps was empowered by the League to keep the interstellar peace, which it did in exemplary fashion. If not always in the most honest way. It has been said that you set a thief to catch a thief—and the Corps personified this ideal. At one time, before joining the Corps, Inskipp had been the biggest crook in the lenticular galaxy; an inspiration to us all. I am forced to admit that I too had led a less than exemplary life before my forced conversion to the powers of goodness. An incomplete conversion, as you may have noticed, though I like to feel that my heart is in the right place. Even if my fingers are not. I took out the blank pistol that I carried for just such occasions and pressed it to the side of my head.

"If you think I should be shot, great Inskipp, then I can but help you. Goodbye cruel world . . ." I pulled the trigger and it made a satisfactory bang.

"Stop horsing around, diGriz. This is serious."

"It always is with you, whereas I believe that a certain amount of levity aids the digestion. Let me take that thread from your lapel."

I did, and slipped his cigar case from his pocket at the same time. He was so distracted that he did not notice this until I lit up and offered him one as well. He snatched the case back.

"I need your help," he said.

"Of course. Why else would you be here fixing charges and such. Where is my darling Angelina?"

"Out of jail and on the way home to curb your larcenous offspring. The morons on this planet may not know what has happened to their tax files but *I* do. However, we will forget that for the moment since a

ship is waiting at the spaceport to take you to Kakalak-
two."

"A drab planet circling a dark star. And what will
I find at this unpromising location?"

"It's what you won't find that counts. The satellite
base there was the site of the biannual meeting of all
planetary chiefs of staff of the League Navy. . . ."

"You said *was* with a certain amount of accentua-
tion. Should I believe . . . ?"

"You should. They have vanished without a trace.
So has the satellite. We haven't the slightest idea of
what happened to them."

"Will they be missed? I should think that a certain
amount of jubilation will be heard below decks—"

"Save the humor, diGriz. If the press gets ahold
of this just think of the political repercussions. Not to
mention the disorganized state of our defenses."

"That shouldn't worry you too much. I don't see any
intergalactic warfare looming on the horizon just now.
In any case—let me call home with a censored version
of this information and off we go."

*Behind the air intake in the wall the creature
hung, supported by sucker-equipped tentacles. It
blinked large green eyes in the darkness and made
muffled chomping sounds as it worked its needle-
sharp red teeth against its bony palate. It stank,
too.*

"There is something fishy here, Slippery Jim, and I
don't like it," my Angelina said, eyes flashing fire from
the viewplate. How I loved her fire.

"Never, my sweet!" I lied. "A sudden assignment,
that's all. A few days' work. I'll be back as soon as it is
done. Now that the boys have graduated you must
get out the old travel brochures and find a nice spot
for us all to go for a holiday."

"I'm glad you mentioned the boys. They slunk in a
few minutes ago all bashed and dirty and tired and
would not say a word as to what had happened."

"They will. Tell them Dad says All Operations Go

and they should tell you the entire story of our evening's interesting adventures. See you soon, my sweet!" I blew her a kiss and switched off before she could protest again. By the time she had heard of the night's nonsense I would be off planet and finishing this intriguing new assignment. Not that I cared much what happened to a few hundred admirals, but the mechanics of their disappearance should prove interesting.

It did. As soon as we were en route to Kakalak-two I cracked open the file, poured a large glass of Syrian Panther Sweat, a guaranteed coronary in every bottle, and sat down for a good read. I did this slowly, then a second time a little faster—then a third just to hit the high points. When I dropped the folder I saw that Inskipp was seated across from me, glaring, chewing his lip, tapping his fingers on the table and swinging his toe up and down.

"Nervous?" I asked. "Try a glass of this—"

"Shut up! Just tell me what you think, what you've found out."

"I've found out that we are going to the wrong place, for openers. Change course for Special Corps Main Station so I can have a chat with my old friend, Professor Coypu."

"But the investigation—"

"Will accomplish nothing on the spot." I tapped the file. "It's all been done already. All of your military types assembled, usual radio traffic—then the warning shouts and the cryptic cry of 'The teeth!,' then nothing more. Your highly trained investigating team went there and found empty space and no remnant of the satellite nor any trace of what had happened. If I go there I would find the same thing. So take me to Coypu?"

"Why?"

"Because Coypu is the master of the time-helix. In order to find out what happened I am going to slip back in time just long enough to see what occurred on that fateful day."

"I never thought of that," Inskipp mused.

"Of course not. Because you fly a desk and I am the

best field agent in the Corps. I will take one of your cigars as a reward for my sterling qualities, so often displayed."

Prof Coypu was not interested. He clattered his impressive yellow buck teeth against his lower lip, shook his head *no* so emphatically that the few remaining long strands of gray hair dropped over his eyes, while at the same time making pushing motions with his hands.

"Are you trying to tell us you don't like the idea?" I suggested.

"Madness! No, never. Since the last time we used the time-helix there has been nothing but temporal feedback along the static synergy curves . . ."

"Please, Professor Coypu," I begged. "Simplify, if you please. Treat me and your good master, Inskipp here, as if we were scientific imbeciles."

"Which you are. I was forced to use the time-helix once to save us all from dissolution, then was prevailed upon to use it again to rescue you from the past. It shall not be used again—you have my word!"

Inskipp proved he was made of sterner stuff than any rebellious physicist. He stepped forward briskly until he and Coypu were in eyeball-to-eyeball contact —or rather nose-to-nose contact since they both had impressive honkers. Once in position he let fire a salvo of drill sergeant oaths followed by some very realistic threats.

"And as your employer if I say *go*—you *go*. Without a trace. You won't be killed, we are not that cruel, but you will be back teaching first-year physics to moronic students on a back water planet so far from the civilized haunts of man that they think time machine means a watch. Going to cooperate?"

"You can't threaten me," Coypu blustered.

"I already have. You have one minute left. Guards!" Two anthropoid brutes in wrinkled uniforms appeared on each side of the little professor and seized him strenuously by the arms so that his toes dangled just clear of the floor. "Thirty seconds," Inskipp sussurated with all the warmth of a striking cobra.

"I've always wanted to run more calibrating tests on the time-helix," Coypu backwatered quickly.

"Fine," Inskipp relented. "Toes on deck, that's it. This will be an easy one. You will flip our friend here about one week back in time, along with the means to return when his mission is accomplished. We will give you the coordinates and time to which he is to be returned. You need know nothing else. Are you ready, diGriz?"

"As ready as I will ever be." I looked at the space suit and the pile of equipment I had assembled. "Suit up and let's get going. I am as eager to see what happened as you are, and even more eager to return since I have done this time travel gig before and it is hard on the system."

The coiled spring of the time-helix glowed greenly, with all the attraction of a serpent's eye. I sighed and prepared myself for the journey. I almost wished that I had submitted myself to the clammy, corpselike embrace of the tax man.

Almost.

FOUR

The mere fact that this was not my first trip through time did nothing to alter the uncomfortable sensations of the journey. Once again I felt the wrenching in a new and undescribable direction, yet again saw the stars whizzing by like rockets. It was very uncomfortable and lasted far too long. Then the sensations ceased as quickly as they had begun, the grayness of time-space vanished to be replaced by a healthy black universe speckled with stars. I floated in null-G, turning slowly, admiring the spectacle of the satellite station as it swung into view. I took a quick bleep with the radar unit on my chest and saw that I was ten kilometers away, just the spot where I should have been. The satellite was a good-sized one, studded with aerial arrays and blinking beacons, its many windows glowing with lights. Filled, I was sure, with rotund admirals swilling and swigging and occasionally doing a bit of military business. But they had a surprise coming which I was looking forward to. I tuned my radio to their time signal broadcast and found I was an hour later than our target time; Coypu would be interested in hearing that. But I still had almost five hours to kill before the moment of truth. For all the obvious reasons I could not smoke a cigar in the spacesuit—but I could still drink. And I had taken the simple precaution of draining the water from the suit's tank and topping it up instead with a mixture of bourbon and water. Some 32,000 years earlier, on a planet named Earth, I had developed a taste for this beverage. Though that planet had long since been destroyed, I had brought back the formula and, after a certain amount of lethal experimentation, had learned to produce a potable imitation. I wrapped my lips around the helmet drinking tube and poted. Good indeed. I admired the brilliant stars, the nearby satellite, recited poetry to myself and the hours flew by.

Just five minutes before the important event was due to happen, I was aware of a sudden movement out of the corner of my eye. I turned to see another space-suited figure floating nearby. Seated on a two-meter-long rocket-shaped object. I whipped out my pistol, I had insisted on bringing it since I had no idea what I would be facing, and pointed it at the newcomer.

"Keep your hands in sight and turn so I can see you. This gun is loaded with explosive shells."

"Put it away, stupid," the other said, back still turned to me while he worked on the control panel of the rocket. "If you don't know who I am no one does."

"Me!" I said, trying not to gape.

"No, I. Me is you, or some such. Grammar isn't up to this kind of thing. The gun, blockhead!"

I closed my jaw with a clack and slid the pistol back into its holster. "Would you mind explaining . . ."

"I had better since you, or I, didn't have enough brains to think of this in the first place so a second trip had to be made. To bring this spacewarp leech along." He looked at his watch, or I looked at my watch or something like that, then he (I?) pointed.

"Keep the eyes peeled—this is really going to be good."

It was. Space beyond the satellite was empty—then an instant later it wasn't. Something large, *very* large, appeared and hurtled toward the satellite. I was aware of a dark, knobbed, elongated form that suddenly split open in the front. The opening was immense, glowing with a hellish light, gaping like a planet-consuming mouth lined with pinnacles of teeth.

"*The teeth!*" my radio crackled loudly, the single message from the lost—or to-be-lost—satellite, then the great mouth was chomping shut and the station vanished from sight in the instant. A streak of fire seared my vision and the white form of the spacewarp leech hurled itself forward at the attacker. None too soon, because there was the sudden shimmer of an operating warp field about the giant shape—then it was gone again.

"What was it?" I gasped.

"How do I know," I said. "And if I did I wouldn't tell you. Now get back so I can get back or you can, I mean—the hell with it. Move."

"Don't bully," I muttered. "I don't think I should talk to myself this way." I triggered the switch on the case of the return time-helix. And, uncomfortably, returned.

"What did you find out?" Inskipp asked as soon as my helmet was opened.

"Mainly that I have to go back a second time. Order up a spacewarp leech and I'll be happy to explain." I decided against going to the trouble of getting out of the suit and putting it on again. So I leaned against the wall and took a long drag on my bourbon pacifier. Inskipp sniffed the air loudly.

"Are you boozing on the job?"

"Of course. It is one of the things that makes the work bearable. Now, kindly shut up and listen. Something really big appeared out of warpspace, just seconds away from the satellite. A neat bit of navigation that I did not think was possible but which obviously is. Whatever it was opened its shining mouth, all lined with teeth, and swallowed the admirals, space station and all . . ."

"It's the drink, I knew it!"

"No it's not and I can prove it because my camera was going all the time. Then, as soon as the thing had had lunch, it zipped back into warpdrive and was gone."

"We must get a spacewarp leech onto it."

"That's just what I told myself who came back with said object and launched it in the right direction." Right on cue the leech was rolled in. "Great. Come on. Coypu, get me and this thing back to five minutes before zero hour and I will be able to get out of this suit. By the way, you were an hour out in my first arrival and I expect better timing on this run."

Coypu muttered over the recalibration, set dials to his satisfaction, I grabbed onto the long white form of the leech and off I went again. The scenario was the same as the first time, only from a different point of view. By the time I had returned from the second trip I had had enough of time travel and wanted nothing more than a large meal with a small bottle of wine and a soft bed for afters. I got all of these, including more than enough time to enjoy them, for almost a week went by before a report came in about the spacewarp leech. I was with Inskipp when the message arrived and he did a certain amount of eye-boggling and squinting at the sheet as if rereading would change it.

"This is impossible," he finally said.

"That's what I like about you, Inskipp, ever the optimist." I plucked the message from his soggy fingers and read it myself, then checked the coordinates on the chart behind his desk. He was right. Almost.

The spacewarp leech had done its job well. I had fired the thing off in time and it had homed on the satellite gobbler and attached itself to whatever the thing was. They had zipped off together into warpspace where the leech simply held on until emerging into normal space again. Even if there had been multiple jumps the leech was programmed to stay close until it either detected atmosphere or the mass of a planet or a space station. At which point it had come unglued and drifted away; it was wholly nonmetallic and virtually undetectable. Once it had arrived it used chemical rockets to leave the vicinity of its arrival while it checked for a League beacon. As soon as it found the nearest one it had warped there and announced its arrival. Needless to say it had taken photographs in all directions when it arrived at its original target area. At that point the computers chortled over the star sights and determined the point in space from which they had been taken. Only this time the answer they came up with was impossible.

"Or very improbable," I said, tapping the chart. "But if the location is correct I have the nasty feeling we are in for some trouble."

"You don't think it was just a coincidence that it was the admirals who got kidnapped?"

"Ha-ha."

"Yes, I thought you would say that."

To understand our problem you have to ponder the physical nature of our galaxy for a moment. Yes, I know it's boring stuff and best left for the astrophysicists and other dull sods who enjoy this sort of thing. But explanation is necessary. If it helps, think of the galaxy as being shaped like a starfish. It isn't really, but that's good enough for this kind of simplistic stuff. The legs and center of the starfish are groups of stars, with some other stars in between the legs, along with space gas and random molecules and such. Hope I haven't lost you because I know I'm confusing myself. *Anyway*, all of the League stars are situated in one arm right up at the top there, sticking straight up. A few other surveyed suns are near the hub and a scattered few more in the arms to the left and right. Got that? Okay. Now it seems that our toothy satellitenapper had come from the way down in the lower left leg.

Well why not, you might say, it's all part of the same galaxy. Well, aha, I say right back. But it is a part of the galaxy we have never been to, have never contacted, have never explored. There are no inhabited planets way down there.

Inhabited by human beings, that is. In all the thousands of years that mankind has been hurtling around the galaxy we have never found another intelligent life form. We have found traces of long-vanished civilizations, but millions of years separate us from them. During the days of colonial expansion, the Stellar Empire, the Feudal Follies and such bits of nonsense, ships went off in all directions. Then came the breakdown and the bustup of communications for many thousands of years. We are coming out of that now. Contacting planets in all states of civilization—or lack of it. But we're not expanding. Maybe we will again, someday, but meanwhile the League is busy picking up the pieces from the first expansion.

Except now there is a new ball game.

"What are you going to do?" Inskipp asked.

"*Me?* I'm going to do nothing except watch you issue orders to investigate this interesting situation."

"Right. This is order one. You, diGriz, get out there and investigate."

"I'm overworked. You have the resources of a thousand planets to draw upon, entire navies, albeit minus the admirals usually in charge, agents galore. Use some of them for a change."

"No. I have the strong feeling that feeding a normal patrol ship into this situation will be like asking them to take a stroll through the guts of an atomic pile."

"A confused description—but I get the message."

"I hope so. You are the crookedest agent I know. You have a sense of survival that, so far, has made you unkillable. I am banking on that and the hideously twisted convolutions of your warped mind to get you through. So get out there and see what the hell is happening, and get back with a report."

"Do I have to bring the admirals back?"

"Only if you want to. We have plenty more where they came from."

"You are heartless and cruel, Inskipp, and as big a crook as I am."

"Of course. How else do you think I run this outfit? When do you leave and what do you need?"

I had to think about that. I couldn't go without telling my Angelina, and once she learned how dangerous it would be she would insist on coming. Fine. I'm a male chauvinist pig at heart, but I know true talent when I see it and I would rather have her with me than all of the rest of the Special Corps. But what about the boys? The answer to that was obvious as well. With their natural bent and inherited characteristics they were fit only for lives of crime or careers in the Corps. They would have to be blooded sometime and this looked very much like the time. So it was settled. I unglazed my eyes and realized that I had been muttering to myself for some minutes and that Inskipp was looking at me in a very suspicious manner and reaching slowly for the scramble button on his desk. I groped through my memory for the question he had asked me before I had sunk into my coma.

"Ahh, yes, hmmm, of course. I leave soonest, I have my own crew, but I want a fully automated grinder-class cruiser with all armaments, et cetera."

"Done. It will take twenty hours to get one here. You have that long to pack and write a new will."

"How charming of you. I will need but one psi call."

I set it up with the communication center who were on to the operator on Blodgett like a flash and a line hooked through seconds later to Angelina.

"Hello, my sweet," I said. "Guess where we are going for our holiday?"

FIVE

"It's a fine ship, Dad," Bolivar said, running his eyes appreciatively over the varied controls of the *L. C. Gnasher*.

"I hope so. These grinder-class cruisers are supposed to be the best in space."

"Central fire controls and all, wow," James said, thumbing a button before I could stop him.

"You didn't have to blast that hunk of space rock, it wasn't doing you any harm," I complained, switching the gun controls to my pilot's position before he could cause any more trouble.

"Boys will be boys," Angelina said, looking on with motherly pride.

"Well, they can be boys with their own pocket money. Do you know how many thousands of credits it costs every time those energy cannon are fired?"

"No, nor do I care." She raised one delicate eyebrow. "And since when have *you* cared, Slippery Jim, plunderer of the public pocket?"

I muttered something and turned back to the instrument displays. Did I really care? Or was it just fatherly reflex? No—it was authority! "I'm captain and the crew can but obey."

"Shall we all walk the plank, dear?" Angelina asked in her most unreasonable tone. I changed the subject.

"Look. If you will all kindly sit over there I will order up a bottle of champagne and a chocolate cake and we will relax a bit before this mission begins and I start cracking the whip."

"You've already told us the whole deal, Dad," James said. "And could you make that a strawberry shortcake?"

"I know you all know all about what has happened and where we are going, but just what we will do when we get there is yet to be determined."

"I'm sure you will tell us in due time, dear. And isn't it a little early in the day for champagne?"

I punched busily at the catering controls and fought to organize my thoughts. All chiefs and no indians in this outfit. I must be firm.

"Now hear this. Order of the day. We blast off in exactly fifteen minutes. We will proceed with all due dispatch to the position in space determined by the spacewarp leech. We will emerge from spacewarp for exactly one point five seconds which will be enough time to make instrument readings of the surrounding volume of space. We will then automatically return to our last position and analyze our findings. We will then act upon them. Understood?"

"You're so masterful," Angelina murmured, then sipped at her champagne. There was no way of telling from her tone of voice just what she had meant by this remark. I ignored it.

"Then forward. Bolivar, I see by your school record that you had good marks in navigation . . ."

"I had to. We were chained to the desks without food until we passed the test."

"Details, details—that is all behind you now. Set up a course to our target area and let me review it before you actuate. James, you will program the computer to take the readings we will need upon arrival and get us out of there in the second and a half we will have."

"And what shall I do, my love?"

"Open the other bottle, my sweet, and we will look on with pride while our offspring work."

And work they did, with no complaints, and each did a fine job. There were no games now. This was reality and survival and they threw themselves into it with gusto. I checked and rechecked the results but could find no faults.

"A gold star for both of you. Take a double portion of cake each."

"It rots the teeth, Dad. We would like some champagne instead."

"Of course. In time for a toast. Here's to success."

We clinked glasses and sipped and I leaned across and pressed the flight button. We were off. Like all voyages there was absolutely nothing to do once the computer had been programmed. The twins prowled the ship with tech manuals until they had learned every detail of her operation. Angelina and I found far more interesting things to do and the days tiptoed by on little golden feet. Until the alarm pinged and we were ready for the last spacewarp. Once again we assembled in the control room.

"Dad, did you know we have two patrol boats aboard?" Bolivar asked.

"I did, and fine little craft they are. Get ready for the quick look as planned. After we suit up in combat armor."

"Why?" James asked.

"Because you have been ordered to do so," Angelina said and there was a steel edge to her voice. "Plus a moment's rational thought would have given you the answer without asking."

Thus reinforced, I felt my authority was firm and said no more while we all suited up. The combat suits, armored and armed spacesuits, would keep us alive if anything nasty was waiting at the other end.

Nothing was. We arrived, all of the instruments buzzed and clicked—and we were back to our starting point a hundred light years' distant. I made everyone stay armored up in case we had been followed, but we had not been. After a half an hour we climbed out of the suits and ran the results of our investigations.

"Nothing really close," Angelina said, scanning the printout. "But there is a star system just two light years' distant."

"Then that's our next target," I said. "The plan is this. We are going to stay right here a nice distance from whatever is out there. But we'll send in a spyeye to chart the system, look for inhabited planets, scout them as well, and send back continuous reports to a satellite receiver in orbit nearby. The satellite will be programmed to return here the instant anything happens to the spyeye. All right?"

"Can I program the spyeye?" Bolivar asked, speaking an instant ahead of his brother. Volunteers! My heart warmed and I gave them their assignments. Within minutes the machines were launched and, once they were on their way, we sat down to dinner. We were just about finished with the meal when the satellite announced its return.

"That was fast," Angelina said.

"Too fast. If something got the spyeye I think they have some pretty good detection equipment. Let us see what it found out."

I speeded up the recording until we got to the busy part. The star in the center of the screen rushed at us and became a burning sun in an instant. The figures on the second screen revealed that the system had four planets and that radiation consistent with communication and industrial activity was coming from four of them. The spyeye headed for the nearest world and skimmed low.

"My, oh my," Angelina whispered, and I could only nod agreement.

The entire planet appeared to be a single fortress. Mouths of great guns gaped upward from thick-walled fortresses; row after row of spaceships were lined up in apparently endless ranks. As the spyeye skimmed along countless war machines rolled up over the horizon. No bit of the planet's natural surface seemed visible, just more and more machines of war.

"There, look," I said. "That looks just like the space-whale that swallowed up the admirals and their satellite. And another of the same—and another."

"I wonder if they're friendly?" Angelina said, and was barely able to smile at her own joke. The boys were goggle-eyed and silent.

The end came quickly. Four sudden blips on the radar, closing at headlong speed—and the screen went blank.

"Not *too* friendly," I said, and poured myself a drink with a none-too-steady hand. "Make a recording of what we discovered and get it started on a relay back to base. Route it by the nearest base with a psiman so a condensed report can get back soonest. Then I would like someone to suggest a next step for us. Once we have made the report of what we have discovered we are on our own again."

"And expendable?" Bolivar asked.

"You're catching on, son."

"Great," James said. "On our own with orders from no one."

I don't know how much he meant it, but I was proud of my sons right then and there. "Any suggestions?" I asked. "Because if not I have the glimmerings of a plan."

"You're the captain, dear," Angelina said, and I *think* she meant it.

"Right. I don't know if you noticed it on the readout, but that star system is filled with spatial debris. I suggest we find the right-sized hunk of rock and hollow it out and slip one of the patrol boats inside. If we shield it correctly there will be nothing to show that is different from the rest of the boulders floating around that system. Then ease it into orbit, check out the other planets, see if there are any satellites we can slip up on, generally get more information so we can plot out a plan of attack. There must be someplace we can get closer to that isn't armed to the teeth like that first planet. Agreed?"

After some discussion—since no one could come up with a better plan—it was. We moved out in space drive, radar blipping, and within an hour had found a cloud of rocks and stone, meteoric iron and interstellar mountains, apparently in elliptic orbit about the nearest star. I eased up slowly to the mass, matching velocities and picking out the one we wanted.

"There," I announced. "Right shape, right size, almost pure iron so it will shield the ship within. Angelina, take the helm and bring us in close. Bolivar, you and I will suit up and slip over there in the patrol boat. We can use its guns to drill the hole we need. James will do communications at this end. Keep in touch with us and send over any special equipment we might need. It should be an easy job."

It was. At minimum output the nose cannon on the patrol boat drilled neatly into the iron, sending out clouds of monatomic gas. When the hole looked deep enough I sealed my suit and went out to examine it for myself, drifting down the length of the silvery drill hole.

"Looks good," I said when I emerged. "Bolivar, do you think you can ease her in, nose first, without breaking off too many pieces of that ship?"

"A piece of cake, Dad!"

He was as good as his word, and I stood to one side as the patrol boat slid silently by and vanished from sight. Now we could plant instrumentation on the surface, connect it through to the ship, cut another hunk of asteroid to plug the hole when we went in, arrange braces for the boat . . .

I was facing the *Gnasher* as I floated there, and she was clearly visible as she stood by two kilometers away at the edge of the spatial debris field. Her ports glowed cheerfully in the interstellar darkness and I looked forward to getting back and getting my feet up after a good day's work.

Then the black form appeared, blotting out the stars.

It was big and fast, very fast, and the mouthlike glowing opening appeared even as it rushed forward. Opening and engulfing the *Gnasher* and closing again—then vanishing. All in an instant while I could only stay mute in paralyzed silence.

Then it was gone. The ship, Angelina, James. Gone.

SIX

I have had my bad moments but this one, without a doubt, was just about bottom. I was frozen there, fists clenched, staring in horror at the spot where the ship had been but an instant before. Up until this time the sticky moments in my life had, for the most part, involved me and me alone. This solitary danger clears the mind wonderfully, and promotes the gushing of the adrenals when instant action is needed for survival. But now I wasn't threatened or in danger, or possibly dead—but Angelina and James were. And there was nothing I could do.

I must have made some sound while thinking this, undoubtedly a nasty one, because Bolivar's voice rang in my ears.

"Dad? What's going on? Is something wrong?"

The tension broke and I dived for the ship, explaining what had happened as I shot into the airlock. He was white-faced but in control of himself when I appeared in the control compartment.

"What do we do?" he asked in a much subdued voice.

"I don't know yet. Go after them of course—but where do we go? We need a plan . . ."

A high-pitched warble sounded from the communication equipment and I bulged my eyes in that direction.

"What is it?" Bolivar asked.

"A general psi-alarm. I've read about it in the training manuals but I never heard of it being used before."

I punched a course into the controls. "As you undoubtedly know, radio waves travel at the speed of light, so that a message transmitted from a station one hundred light years away would take a hundred years to reach us. Not the speediest form of communication. So most messages are carried in ships from point to point. This is also the only form of communication that is exempt from Einsteinian laws. Psi, which appears to be instantaneous. So the psimen can talk to one another, brain to brain, without a time lag. All of the good ones work for the League and most of these for the Special Corps. There are electronic devices that can detect psi communication, but only at full strength and on a simple on-off basis. Every League ship is equipped with a detector like this, though they have never been used except in tests. To make them switch on *every* psiman alive broadcasts the same thought at the same time. The single word—*trouble*. When this psi-alarm is received every ship spacewarps to the nearest broadcast station to find out what is wrong. We're on our way."

"Mom and James . . ."

"Finding them will take some thought—and some help. And, call it a nagging hunch, but I have a feeling that this alarm is not unrelated to this present business we are involved in."

Unhappily, I was right. We broke out near a repeater beacon and the recorded signal instantly blasted out of our radio.

"*. . . return to base. All ships report for orders. Seventeen League planets have been attacked by alien forces in the past hour. Space war has opened on a number of fronts. Report for orders. All ships return to base. All ships . . .*"

I had the course set even before the message had begun to repeat itself. To Corps Main Base. There was no place else to go. Resistance to the invaders would be organized by Inskipp and all of the available information would be there. I will not tell you how we felt as the days rolled by; Bolivar and I found the time bearable only by repeating that if outright destruction were planned the firepower we had seen could have easily demolished the admirals' satellite and our ship. They wanted the people in them alive. They had to. We did not dare think *why* they wanted them. Just that they were prisoners someplace and that we would get there and free them.

I flew the ship by reflex as we broke out of space-warp near the base. Slamming in at maximum G's, reversing at the last possible moment, again at maximum reverse thrust, killing the controls as the magnetic grapples took hold, reaching the port while it was still opening. With Bolivar at my side all of the way. We went through the corridors at the same pace and into Inskipp's office to find him sound asleep and snoring on his desk.

"Speak," I commanded, and he opened a pair of the reddest eyes I have ever seen. Then groaned.

"I should have known. The first time I have tried to sleep in four days and you appear. Do you know what . . ."

"I know that one of those space-whales swallowed my cruiser along with Angelina and James and we have been bucketing back here in a patrol boat for some time."

He was on his feet swaying. "I'm sorry, I didn't know, we've been busy." He staggered to a cabinet and gurgled dark liquid out of a crystal bottle into a glass, which he drained. I sniffed the bottle and gurgled myself the same amount.

"Explain," I ordered. "What's been going on?"

"Alien invasion—and let me tell you that they are good. Those space-whales are heavily armored battle-ships and we have never been able to dent one. We have nothing that can touch them in space. So all we can do is retreat. They've made no planetary landings yet that we know of, just bombardment from space, because our land-based units are strong enough to keep them off. We don't know how long this will last."

"Then we are losing the war?"

"One hundred percent."

"How optimistic. You wouldn't care to tell me who we are fighting?"

"Yes. Them, *these!*"

He flicked on the screen and stabbed the buttons and, in gorgeous color and three-dimensional reality, a loathsome form hung before us. Tentacled, slimily green, clawed and greasy, with far too many eyes sticking out in odd directions, as well as a number of other appendages best left undescribed.

"Uggh," Bolivar said, speaking for all of us.

"Well, if you don't like that," Inskipp growled, "how about this—or this." The slide show of slugs clicked by, creature after creature, each one more loathsome—was it possible?—than the one before. Hideous sqwitchy things, united only in their repugnancy.

"Enough," I finally shouted. "A reducing diet of nausea. I won't eat for a week after this. Which one of them is the enemy?"

"All of them. Let Prof Coypu explain."

The recording of the professor appeared on the screen, and was quite an improvement over the creepy-crawlies despite his gnashing teeth and lecture room manner.

"We have examined the captured specimens, dissecting the dead ones and brain-vacuuming the live ones for information. What we have discovered is rather disconcerting. There are a number of life forms involved, from different planetary systems. From what they say, and we have no reason to doubt them, they are involved on a holy crusade. Their single aim is to destroy mankind, wipe all representatives of our species from the galaxy."

"Why?" I asked aloud.

"You will ask why," the recorder Coypu continued. "A natural question. The answer is that they cannot bear looking at us. They consider us too loathsome to exist. There is much talk about not enough limbs, and we are too dry, our eyes don't stick out on stalks, we secrete no nice slime, important guggy organs are missing. They consider us too disgusting to exist side by side with them."

"They should talk!" Bolivar said.

"Beauty is in the eye of the beholder," I advised him. "But I agree with you in any case. Now shut up and listen to the professor."

"This invasion was carefully prepared," Coypu said, shuffling his notes and rattling his fingernails against his protruding teeth. "Since the invasion we have found many alien life forms lurking in dustbins, air conditioner vents, manholes, flush toilets, everywhere. They have obviously been observing us for a long time and massing reports. The kidnapping of the admirals was the first blow of the invasion, an attempt to disrupt our forces by removing their commanders. This left us very short of admirals, but chief petty officers were put in command of units lacking senior officers and the unit efficiency has doubled. However, we lack real intelligence of the enemy's structures and bases since only small ships have been captured, manned by junior officers. It is suggested that more information be obtained . . ."

"Oh, thanks very much," Inskipp growled, cutting Coypu off in midsuggestion. "I never would have thought of that myself."

"I can do it," I told him, and enjoyed the way the whites—or really the reds—of his eyes appeared as he rolled them in my direction.

"You? Succeed where all of our forces have failed?"

"Of course. I will abandon modesty and tell you that I am the secret weapon that will win the war."

"How?"

"Let me talk to Coypu first. A few questions, then all shall be revealed."

"We're going after Mom and James?" my son asked.

"You betcha, boy. Top priority on the list, and at the same time we shall save the civilized galaxy from destruction."

"Why do you bother me when I must work?" Coypu screeched from the comscreen, sputtering saliva and as red-eyed as Inskipp.

"Relax," I cajoled. "I will solve all your problems for you, as I have done in the past, but I must enlist your aid to do so. How many different species of alien have you discovered so far?"

"Three hundred and twelve. But why . . ."

"I'll tell you in a moment. All sizes, shapes and colors?"

"You better believe it! You should see my night-mares."

"No thank you. You must have discovered the language they use to communicate with each other. Is it difficult?"

"You already speak it. It's Esperanto."

"Come off it, Coypu!"

"You can't scream at me in that tone of voice!" he said hysterically. Then got control of himself, took a pill and shuddered. "Why not? They obviously have been watching us for a long time, learning all about us before they invaded. They would have heard a lot of our languages, then settled on Esperanto just as we did as the simplest, easiest and most efficient form of communication."

"You've sold me. Thank you, Professor. Get some rest because I'll be over there and you are going to outfit me to slip into the alien HQ and discover what is going on and to rescue my family, and maybe the admirals if I get a chance."

"Just what the hell are you talking about?" Inskipp snarled, with Coypu's screened image echoing the same words in an equally repellent tone of voice.

"Simple. At least for me. Prof Coypu is going to manufacture an alien suit, complete with built-in slime-dripper, and I am going to get inside of it. They will welcome me as one of their own. It will be a new kind of loathy who has just heard of their crusade and who is rushing up to enlist. They'll love me. I'm on the way, Professor."

The technicians did a fast but excellent job. They stuffed the computer full of disgusting alien details, tentacles, claws, eye-stalks, feelers, everything, then programmed it to draw pictures of variations. Wow! Even Bolivar was impressed. We put a couple of them together and juggled the result around a bit and came up with one that would suit.

"That's my Dad!" Bolivar said, walking around the thing and admiring it from all angles.

It looked roughly like a miniature tyrannosaurus rex with advanced leprosy and molting fur. A biped for the obvious reason that I was one. The heavy tail, which bifurcated into sucker-tipped tentacles at the end, both balanced the weighty device and contained storage space for the powerplant and equipment. An oversized jaw, just aswarm with yellow and green teeth, adorned the front of the head; a little bucktoothed too like its maker. Ears like a bat, whiskers like a rat, eyes like a cat, gills like a sprat—it really was loathsome. The front split open and I climbed carefully inside.

"The forearms are only lightly powered and fit over your own arms," Coypu said. "But the heavy legs are servopowered and follow the movements of your legs. Watch out for them, those claws can tear a hole in a steel wall."

"I intend to try that. What about the tail?"

"Automatic counterbalance and it wags as you walk. These controls will enable you to thrash it about when you are not walking, make it look realistic. This switch is the automatic twitcher that moves the tail about a bit when you are sitting or standing for a long time. Watch out for this switch—it controls the recoilless seventy-five mounted in the head just between the eyes. The sight is here on your nose."

"Wonderful. What about grenades?"

"The launcher is under the tail, of course. The grenades themselves are disguised as you-know-what."

"A pretty touch. I see you have the warped kind of mind for this sort of business. Now let me close the zipper and you step back while I try it out."

It took a bit of practice to move the hulking thing about naturally, but after a few minutes I got the knack. I stalked about the lab leaving a trail of slime wherever I went, gouging ruts in the steel deck with my claws, swishing my tail and knocking things about, and even poked my head into the firing range to let go a few shots with my headgun. Recoilless or not, I decided, as I took pills for the headache, to save this gun for real emergencies. As I went back to the lab a small treaded robot came out of a doorway and ran over my tail.

"Hey, get rid of that thing," I called out as the PAIN IN TAIL signal flashed on my readout board. I aimed a kick at the robot which it easily dodged. Then it stopped in front of me and the turret with the optic lenses popped open and I found myself staring into Bolivar's smiling face.

"Is one permitted to ask just what the hell you are doing in that thing," one asked.

"Sure, Dad. I'm going with you. Servant-robot to carry your gear. Isn't that logical?"

"No, it is not." I marshalled my arguments and knew, even as I began, that this was one argument I was going to lose. I lost it—and was secretly glad. Although I feared for his safety, I could sure use someone to back me up. We would both go.

"Where?" Inskipp asked, looking with disgust at my alien suit when I climbed out.

"To that armed planet where they took the admirals. And, probably, Angelina and James as well. If it's not their headquarters or main base or some such it certainly will do until the real one comes along."

"You wouldn't care to tell me how you plan to get there, would you?"

"Delighted. In the same patrol boat that we arrived in. But before we go I want the hull blown open fatally, then roughly patched. Knock it about inside a good deal, crunch some of the nonessential equipment to make it look good. Get plenty of blood from the slaughterhouse and sprinkle it all over. And, I don't like to suggest this, but realism is what counts—do you have some spare human corpses?"

"Far too many," he answered grimly. "And you want one or two of them, in uniform, aboard?"

"They may save our lives. I am going to go blasting in with that ship, radio blaring and lights flashing, and volunteer myself and my planet of creepies to the noble cause of humanity-destruction."

"Which you just happened to find out about when your people captured this ship?"

"You catch on quick for someone your age. Get it done at once, Inskipp, because I want to leave about five minutes ago."

Since this mission seemed to be the single ray of hope in the unmitigated gloom of the losing war, we had the best of service. The battered patrol boat was loaded aboard a combat cruiser that blasted off the instant we were aboard. They ferried us to our destination, the nearest safe area to the enemy stars, then chucked us out. I navigated us around a massive cloud of dust, skirted a black hole or two to blur our trail, then scuttled into the arm of the galaxy that held the enemy.

"Ready, son?" I asked, poking my head out through the slit in the alien's neck.

"Ready when you are, Slippery Jim," the robot responded as the turret clacked down and locked into place.

I sealed up and reached out a clawed arm and shook his tentacle. Then got to work. Extra lights had been installed on the hull, of ugly, alien construction, and I switched these on so that we looked like a space-going Christmas tree. I then started the tape of the recently written anthem of my imaginary home planet and began broadcasting it at full volume on 137 wavelengths. Thus prepared we headed leisurely for the armored planet, wafted there on the strains of delightful groaning music.

Sliming and gurgling,
gnashing with crunch.
We're the most sordid,
of the alien bunch.

SEVEN

"*Kiu vi estas?*" the gravelly voice said, the screen lighting up at the same instant to display a particularly repulsive alien physiognomy.

"*Kiu mi estas? Ciuj konas min, se mi ne konas vin, belulo . . .*"

I had decided to be arrogant, secure in a warm welcome, and very flattering—though calling this wormfaced echh "handsome" took some doing. But the

flattery appeared to help, it preened a handful of ten-
drils with a damp tentacle, and continued in a more
friendly tone of voice.

"Come, come, cutey. They may know who you are
at home—but you're a long way from home now. And
there is a war on so we have to obey security regula-
tions."

"Of course, naturally, I am just filled with enthusiasm. Are you *really* fighting a war of extermination
against the dry-stick-pink-black aliens?"

"We're doing our best, gorgeous."

"Well, count us in! We caught this ship sneaking up
on our planet—we have no spacers but fire a mean
combat rocket—and shot it down. We brain-sucked the
survivors, learned their language, and discovered that
all the attractive races in the galaxy had united against
them. We want to join your forces, I am ambassador
—so issue instructions for we are yours!"

"Mighty nice sentiments," the thing slobbered. "We'll
send a ship up to guide you in and the welcoming
committee will make you welcome. But there is one
question, sweety."

"Ask away, handsome."

"With eyes like yours—you are female, aren't you?"

"Next year at this same time I will be. Right now
I'm in neuter state halfway from he to she."

"It's a date then. See you in a year."

"I'll write it in my diary now," I cooed and hung up
and reached for the nearby bottle. But Bolivar the Robot was ahead of me and had poured a large glass
which I sucked at through a straw.

"Am I wrong, Dad," he asked, "or did that refugee
from the sewage works have the hots for you?"

"Unhappily, my boy, you are right. In our igno-
rance my little disguise turns out to be the height of
female pulchritude among the awful-awfuls. We must
make it more loathsome!"

"That will probably make it more sexy."

"You're right, of course." I insufflated feelingly
through the straw. "I'll just have to put up with their
amorous attentions and try to turn it to some benefit."

Our guide ship appeared moments later and I locked

the automatic pilot onto its tail. We floated downward, through unseen minefields and defensive screens, to land on a metal pad inside a large fortress. I hoped this was the VIP field not the prison entrance.

"You'll want your helmet, won't you, Dad," Bolivar said in a robotic tone of voice. Drawing me back from the brink of my sea of black thoughts.

"Right you are, oh good and noble robot." I put on the goldplated steel helmet with the diamond nebula on front and examined my image in the mirror. Delicious. "And best not to call me Dad anymore. It gives rise to some impossible biological questions."

An improbable parade of slithering, hopping and crawling figures slopped up when we appeared through the lock, the Bolivar-robot carrying the carefully constructed alien luggage. One individual in slimy gold braid stepped out of the pack and waved a lot of claws in my direction.

"Welcome, stellar ambassador," it said. "I am Gar-Baj, First Official of War Council."

"A pleasure, I'm sure. I am Sleepery Jeem of Geshtunken."

"Is Sleepery your first name or a title?"

"It means, in the language of my race, He Who Walks on Backs of Peasants With Sharp Claws, and denotes a member of the nobility."

"A remarkable compact language, Sleepery, you must tell me more about it again—in private." Six of his eighteen eyes winked slowly and I knew the old sex appeal was still at work.

"I'll take you up on that my next fertile period, Gar. But for now—it is war! Tell me how things go and what we of Geshtunken can do to aid this holy cause."

"It shall be done. Let me guide you to your personal quarters and explain as we go."

He dismissed the onlookers with the wave of one tentacle, signaling me to follow him with another. I did, with my faithful robot rolling after me.

"The war goes as planned," he said. "You would of course not know, but we have been many years in the planning stage. Our spies have penetrated all of the human worlds and we know their strength down to the last ray gun charge. We cannot be stopped. We have absolute control of space and are now preparing for the second phase."

"Which is . . . ?"

"Planetary invasion. After knocking off their fleet we'll pick off their planets, one by one, like ripe *cerizoj*."

"That's for us!" I shouted, and raked great gouges in the metal flooring with my claws. "We Geshtunken are fighting fools, ready to lead the charge, willing to die in a cause that is just."

"Just what I was hoping to hear from someone as well built as you, claws, teeth and such. In here, if you please. We have plenty of transport ships but can always use experienced troops—"

"We are death-defying warriors!"

"Even better. You will attend the next meeting of the War Council and plans will be drawn up for mutual cooperation. But now you must be tired and want to rest."

"Never!" I chomped my jaws and bit a chunk out of a nearby couch. "I want no rest until the last dry enemy has been destroyed."

"A noble sentiment, but we must all rest sometime."

"Not the Geshtunken. Don't you have a captive or two I could disembowel for a propaganda film?"

"We have a whole load of admirals, but we need them for brainsuck to aid in the invasion."

"Too bad. I pluck legs and arms from admirals like petals from flowers. Don't you have any female prisoners—or children? They scream nice."

This was the 64,000 credit question hidden among all the other rubbish and my tail twitched as I waited for the answer. The robot stopped buzzing.

"It's funny you should ask. We did capture an enemy spy ship that was crewed by a female and a male youth."

"Just the thing!" I shouted, and my excitement was real. "They must need torture, questioning, crunching. That's for me. Lead me to them!"

"Normally I would be happy to. But that is now impossible."

"Dead . . . ?" I said, fighting to turn the despair in my voice into disappointment.

"No. But I wish they were. We still haven't figured out what happened. Five of our best fighting things alone in a room with these two pallid and undersized creatures. All five destroyed, we still don't know how. The enemy escaped."

"Too bad," I said, simulating boredom now with the whole matter, swinging my tail around and scratching its scrofulous tip with a claw. "You have of course recaptured them?"

"No. And that's the strange part. It has been some days now. But you do not wish to be bothered by petty worries. Refresh yourself and a messenger will be sent for you when the meeting is joined. Death to the crunchies!"

"Death to the crunchies yourself. See you at the meeting."

The door closed behind him and the Bolivar-robot spoke.

"Where will you have the bags, mighty Sleepery?"

"Anywhere, metallic moron." I lashed out with a kick that the robot scuttled back to avoid. "Do not bother me with such petty matters."

I walked about the room, singing the Geshtunken national anthem in a shrill voice, managing to cover all parts of the room as I did so. In the end I plopped down and opened the zipper in my neck.

"You can come out and stretch if you want to," I said. "These drips are really most trusting because I can detect no bugs, spies or optic pickups anywhere in these quarters."

Bolivar exited the robot quickly and did some deep knee bends to the accompaniment of cracking joints. "It gets tight in there after a while. What next? How do we find Mom and James?"

"A good question that brings no easy answer to mind. But at least we know that they are alive and well and causing the enemy trouble."

"Maybe they left messages for us—or a trail we could follow."

"We will look, but I don't think so. Anything we

might follow these uglies could as well. Crack out a bottle of Old Thought Provoker from your kit there and see if there is a glass in this dump. And I will think."

I thought hard, but with little results. Perhaps the atmosphere was a bit offputting. The wall hangings were of moldy green over flaking red paint. Half of the room was filled with a swimming-pool-sized mud wallow that brimmed over with steaming gray sludge that burbled and plopped up big bubbles from time to time that stank atrociously. Bolivar went exploring, but after almost being sucked under by the sanitary arrangements and having a quick look at the food supply —he turned as green as my alien hide—he was happy enough to sit and switch channels on the TV. Most of the programs revealed were impossible to understand, though loathsome to a great degree, or if understandable were depressing—like the current battle reports.

Neither of us realized that the TV was also the communicator until a bell pinged and the scene of space bombardment of a helpless planet gave way to the always repellent features of Gar-Baj. Luckily the di-Griz reflexes were still operating. Bolivar dived aside out of the range of the pickup while I kept my back turned while I zipped up my neck.

"I do not wish to disturb you, Jeem, but the War Council meets and wishes your presence. The messenger will show you the way. Death to the crunchies."

"Yeah, yeah," I muffled as his image faded, trying to get my head into the right position among the folds of plastic flesh. A grating sound issued from an annunciator by the door.

"Get that, robot," I said. "Say I'll be there in a moment. Then break out my train."

When we issued forth, the monster who had been sent to fetch me goggled his eyes at the scene. Impressive too since he had a couple of dozen eyes that suddenly protruded a good meter on stalks.

"Lead the way, spaghetti head," I ordered.

He went and I followed—followed in turn by my robot who held the free end of the train that was buttoned about my shoulders. This attractive garment was a good three meters of shining purple fabric picked out with gold and silver stars and edged with heavy shocking-pink lace. Yummy! Luckily I didn't have to look at the thing, but I pitied poor Bolivar who did. I was sure the locals would love it. Not that I needed a train, but it seemed the simplest way to keep Bolivar by me at all times.

The council was impressed, if globbles, slurps and grunts are meant to be flattery, and I went twice around the council chamber before taking the indicated seat.

"Welcome lovely Sleepery Jeem to our War Council," Gar-Baj slobbered. "Rarely has this chamber been graced by such a gorgeous presence. If all the Geshtunken are like you—and good fighters too I am sure—this war will be won on morale alone."

"A propaganda film," something black, damp and repulsive gurgled from the far side of the room. "Let us share our pleasure with the troops in the field and reveal this lovely presence to all. Also let's mention all the extra combat troops we will soon have."

"Great idea! Wonderful!"

There were shouts of acclaim and joy from all sides accompanied by a feverish waving of tentacles, suckers, eye stalks, antennae, claws and other things too repulsive to mention. I almost lost my lunch but smiled and clattered my teeth together to show how pleased I was. I don't know how long this sort of nonsense would have gone on if the secretary-thing had not hammered loudly on a large bell with a metal hammer.

"We have urgent business, gentlethings. Can we get on with it?"

There were angry shouts of "spoilsport"—and worse —and the secretary cringed. It was a repulsive creature, like a squashed frog with a furry tail and a sort of leechlike sucker where the head should be. It flapped its forearms apologetically, but nevertheless went right back to work when the shouting had died down.

"This four thousand and thirteenth meeting of the War Council will come to order. Minutes of the last meeting are available if any of you care. New business is battle order, logistic invasion plans, bombardment reserve management and interspecies food supply availability." The secretary waited until the groans had died away before it continued. "However, before we begin we are asking our new member for a brief speech to be broadcast with the evening news. We are recording, Sleepery Jeem. Will you oblige us with your address . . ."

There was a lot of splattering slopping sounds from many tentacles, which I realized passed for applause, and I bowed into the camera's eye, hitching my train up a bit as I did.

"Dear wet, slimy, soggy friends of the galactic cluster," I began, then waited with eyes lowered coyly until the applause died away. "I cannot tell what pleasure beats in my four hearts to squat here among you today. From the moment we on Geshtunken discovered that there were others like us we oozed with eagerness to join forces. Chance made this possible and I am here today to say that we are yours, united in this great crusade to wipe the pallid pipestems from the face of our galaxy. We are known for our fighting abilities . . ." I kicked a hole through the lectern with the words and everything cheered. ". . . and wish to bring our skills to this holy cause. In the words of our Queen, the Royal Engela Rdenrundt, you can't hold a good Geshtunken down—nor would you want to try!"

I sat down to more excited shouts and crossed my claws, hoping my little ruse had succeeded. No one seemed to have noticed. It was a long shot that might just work. Wherever Angelina was on this planet there was a chance that she might be able to get near a communicator. If so she might watch the news and *if* she did she would certainly recognize the name under which I had first met her, some years ago. A long shot, but better than nothing.

My fellow monsters were not really happy with work, but the sordid little secretary managed to drive them to it eventually. I memorized all the essentials of the various war plans and, being a newcomer, offered no suggestions. Though when I was asked how many combat troops we Geshtunken could field I gave inflated figures that got them all happy again. It went on like this for far too long and I wasn't the only one who cheered when the secretary announced that the meeting was adjourned. Gar-Baj writhed up and laid what I can only assume was a friendly tentacle across my tail.

"Why not come to my place first, cutey? We can crack a crock of rotted slung juice and have a nibble or two of pyekk. A good idea?"

"Wonderful, Gar-baby, but Sleepery is sleepy and must get the old beauty rest. After that we *must* get together. Don't call me—I'll call you."

I swept out before he could answer, the robot rushing after with the end of my train. Down the rusty corridors to the door to my own place, hurrying through it happily to escape the passionate embraces of my loathy Lothario.

But the door slammed shut before I could touch it and a blaster shot burned the floor next to me. I froze as a gravelly voice ground in my ear.

"Move and the next one is right through your rotten head."

EIGHT

"I'm unarmed!" I shouted in a voice just as hoarse as that of my unseen attacker. "I'm reaching for the sky— don't shoot!" Was that voice somehow familiar? Dare I risk a look? I was trying to make my mind up when Bolivar made it up for me. He popped open the robot and stuck his head out.

"Hi, James," he called cheerily. "What's wrong with your throat? And don't shoot that ugly alien because your very own dad is inside."

I risked a look now to see James lurking behind a piece of furniture, jaw and blaster hanging limply with astonishment. Angelina, tastefully garbed in a fur bikini, stepped in from the other room holstering her own gun.

"Crawl out of that thing at once," she ordered, and I

struggled free of its plastic embrace and into her decidedly superior one. "Yum," she yummed after a long and passionate kiss was terminated only by lack of oxygen. "It has been light years since I've seen you."

"Likewise. I see you got my message."

"When that creature mentioned *that* name on the news broadcast I knew you were involved somehow. I had no way of knowing you were inside, which was why we came with the guns."

"Well, you are here now and that is what counts, and I love your outfit," I looked at James's fur shorts, "and James's as well. I see you go to the same tailor."

"They took all our clothes away," James said, in the same rough voice. I looked at him more closely.

"Does that scar on your throat have anything to do with the way you talk?" I asked.

"You bet. I got it when we escaped. But the alien that gave it to me, that's where we got the fur we're wearing."

"That's my boy. Bolivar, crack a bottle of champagne out of our survival kit, if you please. We shall celebrate this reunion while your mother explains just what has happened since we saw her last."

"Quite simple," she said, wrinkling her nose delightfully at the bubbles. "We were engulfed by one of their battleships—I'm sure you saw that happen."

"One of the worst moments of my life!" I moaned.

"Poor darling. As you can imagine we felt about the same way. We fired all the guns but the chamber is lined with collapsium and it did no good. Then we held our fire to get the aliens when they came to get us, but that was no good either. The ceiling of the chamber came down and crushed the ship and we had to get out. That was when they disarmed us. They thought. I remembered that little business you did on Burada with the poisoned fingernails and we did the same here. Even our toenails, so when they took our boots away it helped us. So we fought until our guns were empty, were grabbed, taken to a prison or a torture chamber —we didn't stay long enough to find out—then we polished off our captors and got away."

"Wonderful! But that was endless days ago. How have you managed since?"

"Very well, thank you, with the aid of Cill Airne here."

She waved her hand as she said this and five men jumped in from the other room and waved their weapons at me. It was disconcerting yet I stood firm seeing that Angelina was unmoved by their display. They had pallid skins and long black hair. Their clothing, if it could be called that, was made of bits and pieces of alien skin held together by scraps of wire. Their axes and swords looked crude—but serviceable and sharp.

"Estas granda plezuro renkonti vin," I said, but they were unmoved. "If they don't speak Esperanto what do they talk?" I asked Angelina.

"Their own language of which I have learned a few words. *Do gheobhair gan dearmad taisce gach seoid,"* she added. They nodded in agreement at this, clattered their weapons and emitted shrill war cries.

"You made quite a hit with them," I said.

"I told them that you were my husband, the leader of our tribe, and you had come here to destroy the enemy and lead them to victory."

"True, true," I said, clasping my hands and shaking them over my head while they cheered again. "Bolivar, break out the cheap booze for our allies while your mom tells me just what the hell is going on here."

Angelina sipped at her champagne and frowned delicately. "I'm not sure of all the details," she said. "The language barrier and all that. But the Cill Airne appear to be the original inhabitants of this planet, or rather settlers. They're human enough, undoubtedly a colony cut off during the Breakdown. How or why they came this far from the other settled worlds we may never know. Anyway, they had a good thing going here until the aliens arrived. It was hatred at first sight. The aliens invaded and they fought back, and are apparently still fighting back. The aliens did everything they could do to wipe them out, destroying the surface of this planet and covering it, bit by bit, with metal. It didn't work. The humans penetrated the alien buildings and have lived ever since hidden in the walls and foundations."

"Stainless steel rats!" I cried. "My sympathy goes out to them."

"I thought it might. So after James and I escaped and were running down a corridor, not really sure where we were going, this little door opened in the floor and they popped out and waved us inside. That's when the last alien guard jumped us and James dispatched him. The Cill Airne appreciated this and skinned him for us. Perhaps we couldn't talk their language, but mayhem speaks louder than words. And that's really about all that happened to us. We have been lurking around in wainscottings and putting together a plan to capture one of their spacers. And to free the admirals."

"You know where they are?"

"Of course. And not too far away from here."

"Then we need a plan. And I need a good night's rest. Why don't we sleep on it and do battle in the morn?"

"Because there is no time like the present and besides, I know what you have on your mind. Into battle!"

I sighed. "Agreed. What do we do next?"

That was decided when the door burst open and my paramour Gar-Baj came charging in. He must have had love on his mind, if the pink nighty he was wearing meant anything, so he was a little off his guard.

"Jeem, my sweet—why do you stand there unmoving with your neck open? Awwrrk!"

He added this last when the first sword got him in the hams. There was a brief battle, which he lost quite quickly, though not quickly enough. He was not completely in the room when the fight started and when his tail was cut off, the last bit, equipped undoubtedly with a rudimentary brain of its own, went slithering back down the corridor and out of sight.

"We had better make tracks," I said.

"To the escape tunnel," Angelina cried.

"Is it big enough for my alien disguise?" I asked.

"No."

"Then hold all activity for a few moments while I think," I said, then thought. Quickly. "I have it. Angelina—do you know your way around this monsters' maze?"

"I do indeed."

"Wonderful. Bolivar, it's your chance to walk. Out of the robot and let your mother get in. Brief her on the controls and then go with the others. We'll meet you at whatever place it is you have been staying."

"How considerate," Angelina beamed. "My feet were getting tired. James, show your brother the way and we'll join you later. Better take along some chops from this creature you have just butchered since we have a few more coming to dinner."

"Meaning?" I asked.

"The admirals. We can free them with all this weaponry you have imported and I will lead them to safety in the subterranean ways."

There was instant agreement on the plan. In the di-Griz family we are used to making up our minds rather quickly, while the Cill Airne had learned to do the same in their constant war against the enemy. Some moldering floor coverings were thrown back to reveal a trapdoor that was levered up. I was beginning to think that the aliens were not very bright if they let this sort of thing happen under their very noses, or smelling tentacles or whatever. Bolivar and James dropped into the opening followed by our allies who exited with many shouts of *Scadan, Scadan!*

"It's really quite cozy in here," Angelina said, slipping into place in the robot. "Is there a closed-circuit radio for communication?"

"There is. Circuit thirteen there, a switch near your right hand."

"I've found it," she said, then her voice spoke into my ear. *"You had better lead the way and I'll give you instructions as we go."*

"Your slightest wish sends me forth."

I stomped out into the corridor with the robot scuttling after. The severed section of tail had vanished. I kicked and buckled the metal door until it was jammed into its frame to confuse the pursuit as much as possible, then led the way down the metal corridor.

It was a long, and frankly boring, trip through the metallic city. The aliens did not appear to be good planners and the constructions themselves seemed to have just been added on with little reference to what had come before. One minute we would be walking down a rusty, riveted corridor with a sagging ceiling —and the next would be crossing a mesh-metal field under the open sky. Sometimes the walkways were used as watercourses as well and I would thrash along at great speed propelled by my wildly waving tail. The robot was too heavy for this and could only roll along the bottom. We passed through warehouses, factories —have you ever seen a thousand things like decaying alligators all working drill presses at once?—dormitories, and other locales that defy description. And everywhere were the loathies, chattering away in Esperanto and giving me a big wave as I passed. Very nice. I waved back and muttered curses inside the head.

"I'm getting a little tired of this," I confided to Angelina on our closed circuit.

"Courage, my brave, we are almost there. Just a few kilometers more."

A barred gate did eventually appear ahead, guarded by spear-bearing tooth-rattling creatures who began a great noise when I appeared. They banged their spears on the floor and shouted and chomped so strongly that bits of splintered teeth flew in all directions.

"Jeem, Jeem!" they cried. And "Geshtunken forever! Welcome to our noble cause!" They were obviously all fans of the evening news broadcast and had caught my shtick. I raised my claws and waited until the tumult died.

"Thank you, thank you," I cried. "It is my great pleasure to serve beside nauseating creatures like yourselves, spawn of some loathsome world far out among the decaying stars." They were prone to flattery and cried aloud for more. "During my brief time here I have seen things that creep, crawl, wriggle and flop, but I must say that you are the creepiest, crawlingest, wriggliest and biggest flop I have met yet." Time out for hoarse shouts of repulsive joy, then I got down to business. "We on Geshtunken have seen only one shipload of pallid-crunchies which we instantly butchered by reflex. I understand you have a whole satellite load of them here. Is that true?"

"It is indeed, Jeem the Sleepery," one of them spattered. I saw now that it had gold comets screwed into the sides of its head, undoubtedly denoting high rank of some kind. I addressed my questions in its direction.

"That is good news indeed. Are they in here?"

"Indeed they are."

"You don't have an old damaged one you don't need anymore for me to disembowel or eat or something?"

"Would that I could to please one as cute as yourself, but, alas, no. All of them are needed for information purposes. And after that the roster is already full, highest rank first, with volunteer disembowelers."

"Well, too bad. Is there any chance I can get a peep at them? Know your enemy and all that."

"Just from here. No one is allowed closer without a pass. Just slip an eyeball or two through the bars and you'll see them over there."

One of my fake eyeballs on stalks did have a TV pickup in it and I slithered it through and turned up the magnification. Sure enough, there they were. And a scruffy lot too. They shuffled in little circles or lay on the deck, gray-bearded and gaunt, the rags of their uniforms hanging from them. They may have been admirals but I was still sorry for them. Even admirals were human once. They would be freed!

"Thanks indeed," I said snaking back my eyeballs. "Most kind and I'll remember you in my report to the War Council."

I waved as we retreated and they all waved back and with all those flying tentacles it looked like an explosion in the octopus works.

"I am depressed," I confided to my robot-wife as we rounded the next bend. "No way to get into them that way."

"Be of good cheer," she radioed. *"And let's try the next stairwell. If there is a level below this one then we can penetrate from beneath."*

"My genius," I said, and clattered my claws lovingly on her metallic shoulder. "That is just what we shall do. And I believe that dead ahead is just what we are looking for. But how will we know when we are under the right spot?"

"We will know because I planted a sonic transponder while you were making your political speech to those slugs."

"Of course! You had this in mind all the time. If it were anyone else I would be green with jealousy. But I writhe with pleasure at the ingenuity of my little wife."

"Well, if you do, try not to phrase the praise in such male chauvinist pig terms. Women are as good as men; usually better."

"I stand chastised, robot mine. Lead the way and I shall follow."

We clattered and bumped down a slime-covered stairway into total darkness. Unused—even better. Angelina switched on some spotlights and we saw a massive metal door ahead that sealed off the foot of the stairs.

"Shall I burn it down?" she asked, poking her head out of the robot for a bit of air.

"No. I'm suspicious. Try out your detectors and see if there is any electronic life beneath the surface."

"Plenty," she said, sweeping it carefully. "A dozen alarm circuits at least. Shall I neutralize them?"

"Not worth the effort. Scan that wall there. If it's clear we'll go in around the door."

We did. These aliens really were simpleminded. The burned-open wall led to a storeroom and the wall beyond this opened into the chamber the bugged door was supposed to guard. Easy enough to do for even an amateur cracksman and my opinion of the enemy IQ dropped a few more points.

"So *this* is why they didn't want anyone cracking in here!" Angelina said, flashing her spotlight around.

"The town treasure," I yummed. "We must come back and dip into it when we get a chance."

Mountains of money stretched away in all directions, loot of a hundred worlds. Gold and platinum bars, cut diamonds, coins and notes of a hundred different kinds, money enough to build a bank out of, much less open one. My larcenous instincts were overwhelmed and I kicked open great bags of bullion with my claws and wallowed in the wampum.

"I know that relaxed you," Angelina said indulgently. "But should we not get on with our rescue operation?"

"Of course. Lead on. I am indeed refreshed."

She beeped her subsonic beeper and followed the pointing arrow. It led us through the treasure hoard and, after burning down a few more doors and walls, we reached the indicated spot.

"We're right under a transponder," Angelina said.

"Good." I took a careful sight. "Then the barred gate will be here, and the prisoners just about here." I paced off the distance carefully. "There were some chairs and debris right here, so if we approach from this spot we should be concealed when we come up. Is your drill ready?"

"Whirring and humming."

"Then that's the spot. Go."

The drill arm extended and began grinding into the rusty ceiling. When the drill note changed Angelina switched off all the lights and drilled even slower in the darkness. This time when she dropped the drill a ray of light shone down through the hole. We waited silently—but there was no alarm.

"Let me get one of my eyes through the hole," I said.

By balancing on tiptail and tiptoe I got my body up high enough to extend an eye stalk up through the opening. I gave it a 360-degree scan, then withdrew it.

"Really great. Junk all around, none of the admirals looking in our direction and the guards are out of sight. Give me the molecular unbinder and stand back."

I climbed out of the alien outfit and up onto its

shoulders where I could easily reach the ceiling. The molecular unbinder is a neat little tool that reduces the binding energy between molecules so that they turn to monatomic powder and slough away. I ran it in a big circle, trying not to sneeze as the fine dust rained down, then grabbed the metal disc as I closed the circle. After handing this down to Angelina I put a wary head up through the opening and looked around. All was well. An admiral with an iron jaw and a glass eye was sitting nearby, the picture of dejection. I decided on a little morale raising.

"Psst, Admiral," I hissed, and he turned my way. His good eye widened and his jutting jaw sank in an impressive manner as he spotted my disembodied head. "Don't say a word out loud—but I am here to rescue you all. Understand? Just nod your head."

So much for trusting admirals. Not only didn't he nod his head, but he jumped to his feet and shouted at the top of his voice.

"Guards! Help! We're being rescued!"

NINE

I didn't really expect much gratitude, particularly from an officer, but this was ridiculous. To traverse thousands of light years of space, through dangers too numerous to mention, to suffer the loving embraces of Gar-Baj, all of this to rescue some motheaten admirals, one of whom instantly tried to turn me in to the guards. It was just too much.

Not that I hoped for anything much better. You don't live to be a gray-whiskered stainless steel rat without being suspicious at all times. My needle gun was ready, since I was alert for trouble from the guards, but I was also certainly prepared to get some from the prisoners as well. I flicked the control switch from "poison" to "sleep"—which took an effort of will, let me tell you—and pinged a steel needle into the side of the admiral's neck. He slumped nicely, dropping toward me with arms outstretched as though for one last grab at his savior.

I froze, motionless, when I saw what was revealed on those skinny wrists.

"What's happening?" Angelina whispered from below.

"Nothing good," I hissed. "Absolute silence now."

With a stealthy motion I lowered my head until just my eyes were above the rim of the opening, still concealed by the broken chairs, empty ration boxes and other debris. Had the guards heard the disturbance? Certainly the other prisoners had. Two octogenarian officers tottered up and looked at the sprawled form of their comrade.

"What's wrong? Fit of some kind?" one of them asked. "Did you hear what he shouted?"

"Not really. I had my hearing aid turned off to save the battery. Something about Mards Phelp, Meer Seen Plescu."

"Doesn't make sense. Perhaps it means something in his native language?"

"Nope. Old Schimsah is from Deshnik and that doesn't mean a thing in Deshnikian."

"Roll him over and see if he's still breathing."

They did and I was watching closely and nodded approvingly when my needle dropped from Old Schimsah's neck when they moved him. With this evidence removed it would be a couple of hours at least before he came to and told them what had happened. That was all the time I needed. Plans were already forming in my head.

Dropping back down, I grabbed the disc of metal so recently removed, smeared the edge with lepak glue—stronger than welding—and pushed it back up into place. There was a crunching sound as the glue set and the ceiling, not to mention the floor above, was solid again. Then I clambered back down and sighed heavily.

"Angelina, would you be so kind as to turn on some of your lights and to crack out a bottle of my best whiskey."

There was light, and a sloshing glass, and patient

Angelina waited until it had been lowered from my lips before she spoke.

"Isn't it time you confided in your wife just what the hell is going on?"

"Pardon me, light of my life, I just had a bad moment there." I drained the glass and forced a smile. "It started when I whispered to the nearest admiral. One look at me and he called the guards. So I shot him."

"One less to rescue," she said with satisfaction.

"Not quite. I used a sleeping needle. No one heard what he said so I slipped away and the opening is sealed, but that is not what is bothering me."

"I know you haven't been drinking, but you don't sound too lucid."

"Sorry. It was the admiral. When he dropped over I saw his wrists. There were red marks like scars around both of them."

"So?" she asked in obvious puzzlement—then her face went suddenly pale. "No, it couldn't possibly be?"

I nodded slowly, finding it impossible to smile. "The gray men. I could recognize their handiwork anywhere."

The gray men. Just thinking of them sent a chill down my back—a back, I must add, that is not chill-prone very often. While I am strong and brave and stand up to the physical batterings of life quite well, I, like all of us, find it hard to resist direct assaults on my gray matter. The brain has no defenses once the inputs of the body have been bypassed. Plug an electrode into the pleasure center of an experimental animal's brain and it keeps pushing the button that supplies the electric fix until it dies of hunger or thirst. Dies happily.

Some years ago, while involved in straightening out a little matter of interplanetary invasion, I had been cast in the role of experimental animal. I had been captured and secured—and had seen both of my hands cut off at the wrists. Then had lost consciousness and, when I came to, had seen the hands apparently sewn back on. With scars just like those the admiral had been sporting.

But my hands had never been cut off. The scene had

been imprinted directly into my brain. Yet for me it had *happened,* along with a number of other loathsome things which are better forgotten.

"The gray men must be here," I said. "Working with the aliens. No wonder the admirals are cooperating. Being firmly structured in the physical world of commands and obedience, they are perfect targets for brain stomping."

"You must be right—but how is it possible? The aliens hate all humans and certainly wouldn't work with the gray men. Nasty as they are, they are still human."

As soon as she said it that way I saw the answer clearly. I smiled and embraced her and kissed her, which we both enjoyed, then held her at arm's length since she was a great distraction to clear thought.

"Now hear this, my love. I think I see a way out of this entire mess. All of the details aren't clear—but I know what you must do. Could you bring the boys and a crowd of those Cill Airne back here? Go up through the floor, shoot the guards, put the admirals to sleep, then carry them away?"

"I could arrange that, but it would be a little dangerous. How would we get them clear?"

"That's what I will take care of. If I had this entire planet in a turmoil, no one knowing what was happening next or who to take orders from or anything—would that make the job easier?"

"It would certainly simplify things. What do you plan to do?"

"If I told you you might say that it was too dangerous and would forbid me. Let me say only that it must be done and that I am the only one to do it. I am off in my alien disguise and you have two hours to assemble the troops. As soon as things start falling apart make your move. Get them all to some safe spot, preferably near the spacedrome. I'll get back to my sleeping quarters as soon as I can. Have a guide waiting there for me. But make sure that he knows that he is to wait no more than one hour for me to show up. What I have to do will be done by that time and I will get back. There should be no problems. But if there is and I'm not there he is to report right back to you. I can take care of myself as you know. And we can't jeopardize everything by waiting for one person. When the guide reports back, with or without me, you go. Grab a spaceship then at the height of the confusion and leave this place."

"And about time too. I'll expect you back." She kissed me but did not look happy. "You're not going to tell me what you are going to do?"

"No. If I told you I would have to listen too and then I might not do it. But it does involve three things. Finding the gray men, turning them over to our alien friends—then getting out of it myself."

"Well, you do that. But don't skip any of the steps— particularly the last one."

We climbed into our various disguises and departed quickly before we changed our minds. Angelina clattered off with knowledgeable tread and I thudded off in the opposite direction. I thought I knew the way but must have made a wrong turning. Looking for a shortcut back to the upper levels, I managed to fall through a rusted plate in the decking into what must have been a covered-over lake or underground reservoir. In any case I thrashed on for quite a while in the darkness, my course lit only by my glowing eyes, until I found the far end. There was no obvious way out but I settled that by dropping a grenade from my cloaca and flicking it against the wall with a twitch of my tail. It crumpled nicely and I crawled through the smoky opening back into the light of day. Just in time to see an officer with a patrol of nasties trotting up to see what was the trouble.

"Help, oh help, please," I moaned, staggering in small circles with my claws pressed to my forehead. Thankfully, the officer was also a TV-news watcher.

"Sweet Sleepery—what is bothering you?" it cried aloud emotionally, showing me about five thousand rotten fangs and a meter or two of damp purple throat.

"Treachery! Treachery in our midst," I cried. "Send a message to your CO to order an emergency meeting of the War Council—then take me there at once."

It was done instantly, and they took me at my word by wrapping a thousand sucker-tipped tentacles around me and rushing me off my feet. This made the trip easier, and saved my batteries, and I was refreshed and relaxed when they finally dropped me at the door to the conference room.

"You are all repugnant lads, and I shall never forget you," I shouted. They cheered and slapped their suckers against the deck with wet shlurping sounds and I galloped into the conference.

"Treason, treachery, betrayal!" I cried.

"Take your seat and make your statement in the proper form after the meeting is correctly opened," the secretary said. But a thing like a purple whale with terminal hemorrhoids was more sympathetic.

"Gentle Jeem, you seem disturbed. We have heard that there has been mayhem in your quarters, and all we can find of the noble Gar-Baj is his tail which doesn't say very much. Can you elucidate?"

"I can—and will, if the secretary will let me."

"Ohh, get on with it then," the secretary grumbled ungraciously, looking more and more like a squashed black frog with every passing moment. "Meeting called to order, Sleepery Jeem speaking re certain grave charges."

"It's like this," I explained to the attentive War Council. "We of Geshtunken have certain rare abilities —in addition to being inordinately sexy, I mean." They appreciated this last and there was a lot of squishy banging on the furniture and wet smacking sounds. "Thank you, and the same to you. Now one thing we can do is smell very good—yes, I know, we smell *good* too, sit down, boy, you're in the way. As I was saying, my keen sense of smell led me to believe that there was something not strictly kosher about this planet. I sniffed out *humans!*"

Through the cries of shocked horror I heard shouts of "Cill Airne!" and I acknowledged them with a nod of my head.

"No, not the Cill Airne, the natives of this planet. I detected their traces at once, but they are like mouse droppings and I know the extermination corps is surely taking good care of them. No, I mean humans right here in our midst! We have been penetrated!"

That rocked them back and I let them shout and writhe a bit while I sharpened my claws with a file. Then I raised my paws for silence and there it was in an instant. Every eye, large, small, stalked, green, red or soggy, was on me. I walked slowly forward.

"Yes. They are among us. Humans. Doing their best to sabotage our lovely war of extermination. And I am going to reveal one to you—*right now!*"

My legs' motors hummed and my power plant grew warm as I sprang into the air with a mighty leap. Sailing in an arc through the air, twenty meters or more. Graceful too. Landing with a horrible crunch that set my shock absorbers groaning. Dropping down crash onto the secretary's desk which crushed nicely. Paws extended so that my claws sank through the secretary's damp black hide. Picking him up and waving him about as he writhed and shouted.

"You're mad. Let me down! I'm no more human than you are!"

That was what made my mind up. Up until this moment it had all been guesswork. The gray men were here, they must be disguised, and the only four-limbed creature other than myself was the secretary. In the position of power to run things, the only really organized alien I had yet encountered. But it was still just guesswork until he had spoken. Roaring with victory I hooked a recently sharpened claw into the front of his throat.

Dark liquid spurted out and he screamed hoarsely.

I gulped and almost hesitated. Was I wrong? Was I going to dismember the secretary of the War Council right in front of the council itself? I had a feeling they would not take that too well. No! It was for only a microsecond that I hesitated—then I tore on. I had to be right. I ripped out his throat, delicately sliced all around his neck—then tore his head off.

There was a shocked silence as the head bounced and squashed on the floor. Then a gasp from all sides.

Inside the first head there was another head. A

small, pallid, scowling human head. The secretary *was* a gray man.

While the council was shocked into immobility the gray man was not. He pulled a gun from a gill slit and leveled it at me. Which of course I had been expecting and I brushed it aside. I was not as quick when he grabbed out a microphone from his other gill and began shouting into it in a strange language.

I wasn't as fast because this was just what I wanted him to do. I gave him more than enough time to get out the message before I grabbed away the microphone. Then he kicked out and got me in the stomach and I folded, gasping and unmoving as he vanished through a trapdoor in the floor.

Recovering quickly I waved away all offers of aid.

"Care not for me," I croaked, "for the blow was mortal. Avenge me! Send out the alarm to grab all the other black ploppies like the secretary. Let none escape! Go now!"

They went, and I had to roll aside before I was trampled in the rush. Then I thrashed and expired, in case anyone was watching, and peeked through one half-closed eyelid until they were all gone.

Only then did I blow open the locked trapdoor and follow the gray man.

How could I follow him? it might be asked, and I will be happy to answer. During the struggle I had stuck a little neutrino generator into his artificial hide, that is how. A zippy neutrino can pass, undeflected and unstopped, through the entire mass of a planet. The metal of this city's construction would surely not interfere with them in the slightest. Need I add that I had a directional neutrino detector built into my snout? I never go on a mission without a few simple preparations.

The illuminated needle pointed that way, and down. I went that way, and down at the first stairwell, because I wanted to find out just what the gray men were doing on this planet. My fleeing secretary would lead me to their lair.

He did one better than that. He led me to their ship.

When I saw light ahead I treaded more slowly, then peered from the darkness of the tunnel at a great domed chamber. In the center was a dark-gray spacer. While from all sides the gray men were appearing. Some running, undisguised, others still hopping and splotching in their alien garb. Rats leaving a sinking ship. All my doing. The confusion across the planet would now be at its height—and the admirals would be rescued. All working according to plan.

Though I hadn't thought to find their ship. From the look of it they were making a hasty withdrawal, and this was too good an opportunity to miss. How could they be traced? There were machines that could be attached to make following the ship easy but, just for a change, I didn't have one on me. An oversight. Particularly since the smallest weighed about ninety kilos. So what could I do?

My mind was made up for me when the metal net dropped and they swarmed all over me.

I was fighting, and doing well, when someone started on my head with a metal bar. I couldn't move it away and the alien head got crushed in.

Mine, too, an instant later.

TEN

I woke up, gasping for air, muffled, trapped, blind. With the super headache of all time. Where I was, what had happened—I had no idea. I thrashed and writhed ineffectually until it made my head hurt more and I had to stop.

Little by little I dropped the mad-panic approach and tried to figure out what the situation was. First off, I wasn't really choking to death; it was just the soft fabric over my head that had made me feel that way. If I lifted my face and turned it I could breathe all right.

So what had happened? Through the waves of skull pain, memory finally returned. The gray men! They had trapped me in a net, then beat on my head until I had stopped moving. After that, blackout. What after that? Where did they have me?

It was only when I had tiptoed this far down memory lane that I realized where I was. I had been bashed and caught in my alien disguise. Apparently I was still bashed and caught in it. My arms were secured inside the mechanical arms, but by careful wriggling—and ignoring the effect this had on my head—I managed to get my right arm free and back inside the suit. With this I pulled the folds of plastic from in front of my face and realized that my head had slipped down inside the neck of the disguise. By wriggling and pushing even more I got my head further up near the optic unit and looked out at a metal floor. Very revealing. I tried moving my other arm and my legs but they twitched, nothing more. It was all very confusing and I was thirsty and sore and the aching head was still there.

Some bit of keen foresight had caused me to install a small spare tank next to the main water one. I found the nozzle for the water, drank all I needed, then threw the switch with my tongue that changed the liquid supply over to life-sustaining 110 proof whiskey. This woke me up quickly enough and, if it did nothing for the hammers in my head, it at least enabled me to ignore them a bit more easily. If I couldn't move very much, at least I should be able to manipulate the eye controls. With some difficulty I got the one out on the stalk functioning and turned it around in a circle.

Interesting indeed. I very quickly saw that the reason I could not move was because heavy chains secured me solidly to the steel floor. They had been welded into place so there was little chance of escape. The room I was in was small and featureless, except for the rust on the metal and the fact that the ceiling was curved, concave. This reminded me of something and another suck at the whiskey unearthed the fact.

Spaceship. I was inside a spaceship. *The* spaceship I had seen just before the lights went out. The gray men's ship and, undoubtedly, no longer grounded but in space and on the way somewhere. I had a good idea just where but I did not want to think about that depressing thought just yet. There was an unsolved question that had to be answered first. Why had they secured me inside my disguise?

"Because, dummy, they didn't know it was a disguise!" I shouted. And instantly regretted it since my head echoed like a drum.

But it had to be true. The alien outfit was a good one designed to bear the closest inspection. They had jumped me and knocked me out. At no time had they any clue that I was other than what I pretended to be—just one more alien ugly. And they must have been in a big hurry; the crude welds that held the chain showed that. They had to leave the war planet before a couple of million slimy monsters dropped on them and ate them. Pack me aboard, weld me into place, blast off for an unknown destination, then take care of me later.

"Whoopee!" I shouted in the tiniest whisper. Then went to work to get out of the disguise.

It was a hard wriggle but I made it, crawling out through the open neck like a newborn moth from a chrysalis. I stretched and cracked my joints and felt much better. Better still when I had abstracted my needle gun from the disguise. Now, standing on the metal deck, I could feel the slight vibration of the drive. We were in space and going somewhere. Free of my chains, with a sturdy gun in my hand, I could face the fact I had ignored earlier. The odds were at least ten to one that we were going home. To the planet of the gray men.

That was not a very nice prospect—but the odds were also good that I could do something about it. Now, well before we landed and before someone came to see how I was doing. They would be tired, bashed about after their escape, possibly off guard. What I had to do must be done soonest. Which was fine by me. I switched the needle gun from "explosive" to "poison" —then on to "sleep." While I was sure that the gray men deserved killing a thousand times over I just could not do it in cold blood. No executioner I. Knocking them out would do just as well for now. If I captured the ship I could chain them all and lock them up. If I didn't win, the number of enemies remaining would make little difference.

"Onward, Slippery Jim diGriz, savior of mankind," I said to cheer myself up. Then was instantly depressed again when I tried the handle on the small door and found it securely locked. "Thermite, of course, how could I be so forgetful," I chided, and went back to the alien outfit. The dispenser still worked and a grenade plopped out and dropped to the deck. Then it was simply a matter of activating the sticky molecules on the end, pressing it to the lock—and setting it off. It burned nicely, filling the small room with a ruddy glow and plenty of dense smoke. Which would have started me coughing if I had not grabbed my adam's apple and squeezed. Gasping, gurgling and turning purple I kicked the still glowing door with my boot and it swung open. I dived right after it, through and rolled and fell flat and poked the gun about in all directions. Nothing. An empty corridor, dimly lit. I permitted myself a single strangled cough which made me feel much better. Then I used the gun barrel to push the door shut again. Only a small warping of the lock on the outside revealed anything wrong. And a closed door might give me the extra moments I needed.

Which way? There were numbers stenciled on the doors and, if this were like a normal spacer, they would get lower in the direction of the bow and the control compartment. I went that way, toward the safety door in the bulkhead which opened as a man stepped through. A gray man. He looked up at me, eyes wide and mouth wider as he started to call out. My needle got him in the throat and he folded nicely. I crouched, ready, but the corridor beyond was empty. So far so good.

Pulling him through and closing the door again took but a moment. Now where should I stow the body? While puzzling over this one I quietly opened the nearest door and peeked into an even more dimly lit sleeping cabin. And that's just what they were doing, a good dozen of the gray men, snoring away like troopers. They slept even more soundly after I had shot them. I dragged the original sleeping beauty in from the corridor and dumped him on a pile of discarded black alien disguises.

"Rest nice," I told them as I shut the door. "You have had a long day, which is going to be even longer before I get you all back for trial."

I could not have been unconscious very long. The discarded disguises and snoring men indicated that we had not been spaceborne for more than a few hours. There would be a crew manning the ship and the rest would be pounding the pillow. Should I try and find them all and put them into a sounder sleep? No, too dangerous, since there was no way of knowing how many there were aboard. And I could be surprised at any time and the alarm sounded. Far better to take the control room as soon as I could. Seal it off from the rest of the ship, then head for the nearest League station and call for help. If I could let them know where I was I could always immobilize the ship and hold out until the cavalry arrived. Great idea. Put it to work.

Gun ready, I tramped the corridors to the control end of the ship. There was a door labeled "communications" and I opened it and said good night to the man at the companel. He slumped and slept. Then the last door was before me. I took a deep breath. My flanks and rear were secured. The end of the job was in front of me. I let the breath out slowly, then opened the door.

The last thing I wanted was a shoot-out since the odds certainly were not in my favor. I stepped in and closed the door and locked it behind me before I counted the stations. Four of them—and all four occupied. Two necks were visible and I needed them and their owners relaxed. I stepped forward silently. The man in the flight engineer's position looked around and caught a needle for his trouble. One remaining. The commander. I didn't want to needle him since I wanted some conversation. Slipping the gun into my belt I stepped forward on tiptoe and reached for his neck.

He turned at the last moment—warned by something—but he was a little too late. I got the grip and my thumbs dug deep. His eyeballs bulged quite charmingly as he thrashed and kicked about for some seconds before going limp.

"Score sixteen to one for the good guys!" I cackled with pleasure, then did a little war dance around the room. "But finish the job, you daring devil, before celebrating too much."

I was right, and I usually gave myself good advice. A drawer in the engineer's desk yielded up a strong roll of wire which I used to secure the commander's wrists and ankles, then added some more turns to tie his wrists to a pipe far from any controls. The other three men I laid out in a neat row beside him, before I tapped some questions into the computer.

It was a nice computer that worked hard to be co-operative. First it gave me our course and destination, which I memorized, and wrote down inside my wrist in case I forgot. If this destination was what I thought it was, then it had to be the home planet of these nasties. The Special Corps would be eager to know just where it was. They had a lot coming to them and I looked forward to helping deliver it. Then I asked for League bases, found the nearest, punched for a course, set it in and relaxed.

"Two hours, Jim, two short hours. Then the warp-drive cuts out and we will be within radio distance of the base. One brief radio message and that is the end of the gray men. Whoopee and chortle, chortle!"

Something itched my neck, someone looking at me, and I turned and saw that the commander was awake and glowering in my direction.

"Did you hear that?" I asked. "Or should I repeat it?"

"I heard you," he said, in a drab, dull voice. Empty of emotion.

"That's good. My name is Jim diGriz." He remained silent. "Come, come, your name. Or do I have to look at your dogtags?"

"I am Kome. Your name is known to us. You have interfered with us before. We will kill you."

"How nice to know that my reputation goes before me. But don't you think your threat has an empty ring?"

"In what manner did you discover our presence?" Kome asked, ignoring my question.

"If you really want to know, you gave yourselves away. You people may be nasty but you have little imagination. The wrist-chopping-off routine works well —I should know—so you keep on using it. I saw the marks on one of the admirals' wrists."

"You did this alone?"

Who was questioning whom? But I might as well be polite considering our positions. "If you must know I am all alone now. But in a few hours the League will be onto you. There were four of us back there with the goppies. All of whom I am sure have escaped now, along with the admirals you treated so badly. They will report what has happened so you will have a nice reception committee waiting when you arrive. You and your people have not been very nice."

"You are telling the truth?"

I lost my temper at this and treated him to some words he had never heard before. I hope.

"Kome, my friend, you are making me lose my temper. I have no reason to lie to you since I hold all the cards. Now if you will shut up and stop asking me questions I will ask you some of my own because there are things I would dearly like to know. Ready?"

"I think not."

I looked up startled, because he had raised his voice for the first time. Not in a shout, there was no anger or feelings in the words. He just spoke loudly, commandingly.

"This farce is at an end. We have found out what we need to know. You may all come in now."

It was very much like a nightmare come alive. The door opened and gray men began to shuffle in slowly. I shot them but they kept coming. And the three officers I had placed on the floor stood up and came toward me as well. I emptied the gun, threw it at them and tried to run.

They grabbed me.

ELEVEN

Good as I am at dirty fighting, hand-to-hand combat and general closeup nastiness, there is a limit. The limit being an apparently inexhaustible supply of the enemy. To make matters worse they really weren't very good fighters. About all they did was grapple. It was enough. I knocked back the first two, slugged the next few, chopped a couple more—and they kept on coming. And, frankly, I was beginning to get tired. In the end they simply swarmed over me and overwhelmed me and that was that. Shackles were clicked into place around my wrists and ankles and I was tossed onto the control room floor. The sound led the battered away and the officers went back to their positions at the controls. Changing my course back to the original one, I noted with dark depression. When he had done this, Kome turned his chair about to face me.

"You tricked me," I said. Not a bright remark but something that might get the conversation rolling.

"Of course."

Laconic was the name of the game with the gray men. Never use a word when none would do. I pressed on, mainly out of a feeling of slight hysteria since I knew I was trapped and trapped well.

"You wouldn't mind telling me why? If you can spare the time, that is."

"I thought it would be obvious. We could of course use our normal mind control techniques on you, and this is what we originally planned to do. But we needed answers to some important questions at once. We have worked among the aliens for years and they have suspected nothing. We needed to know how you had discovered our presence. We of course have psychcontrol techniques for all races. It was when we were preparing brain attachments that we discovered your real identity. Metal skulls do not exist in nature. Your disguise

73

was revealed. Your face resembled very much that of someone we have been searching for for many years. That was when I determined to use this ruse. If you were the man we were looking for we knew that your ego would not permit you to think that you had been tricked."

"Your mother never met your father," I sneered. A feeble response but the best I could do at the moment. Because I knew that he was right. I had been fooled right down the line.

"I knew that if you thought you had the upper hand you would answer questions that might take days to get out of you by other means. And we needed some instant answers. So we arranged the scene you played so well. Your hand weapon was charged with sterile needles. Everyone acted his role well. You best of all."

"I bet you think you're smart" was all I could come up with since, at that moment, I was feeling very defeated.

"I know I am. I have been organizing our field operations for many years—and they have only failed twice. You were to blame each time. Now that you have been captured your interference is at an end." He signaled to two of his men, who picked me up. "Lock him away until we land. I do not wish to speak with him any longer."

Low? Up until that moment I had never known what low was. Depressed, dispirited, out-thought, out-fought, it was enough to bring out the suicidal in anyone. Except me, of course. Where there is life there is hope. Eureka! I was even more depressed after this minor surge of rebellion because I knew this time there was just no hope at all.

These people were too efficient. They hung my wristcuffs over a hook high on the wall and cut away my clothes, boots, everything, in a calmly depressing way. Then they cleaned me out, efficiently, operating like a vacuum cleaner klyster. All of the obvious devices, picklocks, grenades, blades, saws, were stripped from me first. Then they went over me again slowly with fluoroscopes and metal detectors removing, painfully, those other devices that were better hidden. They even X-rayed my jaws and removed a few teeth that had never been discovered before. When they were done I was pounds lighter and as bereft of helpful gadgetry as a newborn babe. It was all quite humiliating. Particularly when they took everything away and just left me lying there, naked, on the cold deck.

Which, I discovered, was getting colder all the time. When moisture began to condense on it I found myself growing blue and chattering with the chill. I began to howl and thrash about. This warmed me up a bit and eventually led to one of the gray men poking his head in the door.

"I am freezing to death!" I clattered through trembling teeth at him. "You are deliberately chilling the air to torture me."

"No," he answered with utmost blandness. "That is not one of our tortures. This ship was warmed when the ports were open and is now returning to normal temperature. You are weak."

"I am freezing to death. Maybe you chilly chaps from your icebox world can live at this temperature— but I can't. So give me some clothes or kill me quickly now."

I think I half meant it. There really did seem to be little left to live for at this point. He thought about it for a bit, then exited. But returned fairly soon with four helpers and a padded coverall. They took off the fetters and dressed me. I made no protests while this was happening because one of them held a fully charged pistol, the muzzle of which he put directly into my mouth. His finger was bent, the trigger half pulled. I knew he meant it. I did not move or twitch while I was being dressed and the heavy boots slipped over my feet. The gun stayed there until the locks on the cuffs clicked shut once more.

It took days to reach our destination. My captors were the worst conversationalists in the galaxy and refused to respond to even my wittiest and most insulting sallies. The food was completely unpalatable but, I am sure, nourishing. The only drink was water. A portapotty took care of my sanitary needs and I was getting bored out of my skull. My thoughts were con-

stantly on escape and many and fearful were the plans
I devised. All of them useless, of course. Singlehanded,
without a weapon, I would never be able to take control of the ship even if I could break out of this room.
Which I could not. I was sinking into a coma of boredom by the time we finally landed.

"Where are we?" I asked the guards who came to
get me. "Come on you chatterboxes, speak up. Would
you be shot if you at least told me the name of the
planet? Do you think I will tell anyone else?"

They thought about this for quite a while until one of
them finally made up his mind.

"Kekkonshiki," he said.

"You're excused—but don't wipe your nose with the
back of your hand. Ha-ha." I had to laugh at my own
sallies. No one else would.

But it was ironic. Here I was, bearer of the information that would put an end to the gray men menace
forever. The name of their world—and its location.
And I couldn't pass it on. If I had any trace of psi
ability I could have the troops rushing there in a minute. I did not. I had tried and been psi-tested often
enough in the past. There was absolutely nothing that
I could do.

At least the unaccustomed action gave me something
new to think about, to take my mind off of the depression that had depressed me for days. At last it was
time to think about escape again.

Nor was I mad to consider it at this time. We had
landed and would be leaving the ship soon. They were
taking me some place where it was guaranteed not-
very-good things would happen to me. I did not yet
know what they were and, as far as I was concerned,
life would be far more peaceful if I never found out. We
would leave this ship, and even for a very brief spell,
we would be in transit. That would be the time to act.
The mere fact that I did not have the slightest idea of
what would be waiting outside was completely and
totally beside the point. I had to do something.

Not that they made it very easy for me. I tried to
act indifferent when they stripped off my chains and
produced a metal collar and snapped it around my

neck. Although my blood ran chill on the instant. I had worn that collar before. A thin cable ran from the collar to a small box that one of them held in his hand.

"No need to demonstrate," I said in what was meant to be a light and bantering tone and certainly was not. "I've worn one of these before and your friend Kraj— you must remember Kraj?—demonstrated its working to me over quite a period of time."

"I can do this," my captor said, poising a finger over one of the many buttons on the box.

"It's been done," I shouted, pulling back. "Those very same words, I know, you never change your routines. You press the button and . . ."

Fire washed over me. I was blind, burning to death, my skin aflame, my eyes seared out. Every one of my pain nerves switched on to full by the neural currents generated by the box. I knew this but it did not help. The pain was real and it went on and on and on.

When it ended I found myself lying on the floor, curled up, drained of energy and almost helpless. Two of them lifted me to my feet and dragged me, legs flopping, down the corridor. My master with the box walked behind, giving me a little tug on the neck from time to time to remind me who was in charge. I did not argue with him. I could stumble along by myself after a bit, but they still kept their hands locked tight on my arms.

I liked that. I fought hard not to smile. They were so sure I could not escape.

"Getting cold out?" I asked when we reached the airlock. No one bothered to answer me. But they were pulling on gloves and fur hats which certainly meant something. "How about some gloves for me?" I was still ignored.

When the lock door swung open I knew why the preparations. A swirl of snow was blown in on a wave of arctic air that chilled, then numbed. It certainly wasn't summer outside. I was dragged forth into the blizzard.

Maybe not a blizzard, but some very heavy flurries. There was a blinding wave of flakes about us that was gone in a few moments. A thin sun shone down on the blindingly white landscape. Snow, nothing but snow in all directions. Wait, something dark ahead, a stone wall or building of some kind, obscured an instant later. We plodded on and tried to ignore the numbness in my hands and face. Yet our destination was still a good two hundred meters away. My body and feet were warm enough, but my exposed skin was something else again.

We were roughly halfway from the ship to our waiting warm haven when another miniblizzard swept down upon us, a roaring snow squall. Just before it hit I slipped and fell, pulling one of my captors down with me as he slid on the icy surface. He made no complaints, though the sadist holding the torture box did give me a quick blast of pain as a warning to watch my step. All done in silence. Silence on my part too because I had managed to get a loop of cable from the box over my shoulder when I went down and then caught it in my mouth. And bit it in two.

This is not as hard to do as it sounds, since under the caps of my front teeth were set serrated edges of silicon carbide. They were invisible to X-ray, having the same density as the enamel of my teeth—but were as hard as tool steel. The caps on my teeth chipped and splintered away as I ground down, chewing desperately before anyone noticed what was happening. The swirling snow concealed what I was doing for the vital seconds needed. The human jaw muscles can exert thirty-five kilos of pressure on each side and I was exerting, chomping and biting to my utmost.

The cable parted. As it did I twisted to the side and brought my knee up into the groin of the captor on my right. He grunted loudly and folded and released my arm. For a quick cross chop into the throat of the other man. Then my hands were free and I spun about.

The man behind me lost vital seconds depending on technology rather than on his reflexes. My back was to him all the time I was chopping up his partners. And he did nothing. Nothing that is other than push wildly at the buttons on the torture box. He was still pushing when my foot caught him in the pit of the stomach. As he fell I got under him so he collapsed onto my shoulder.

I did not stop to see who was doing the yelling as I staggered off with him into the snow-filled, storm-beaten, frozen wastes.

All of this may seem like madness—but what greater madness to go quietly to the slaughter at the hands of these creatures? I had been there once before and still had the scars. Now there was a good chance I would freeze to death. But that was also better than giving in to them. Plus the very remote chance that I might stay free for a while, cause them trouble, anything.

Nor was I as weak as I pretended to be; this had been only a simple ruse to get them off guard. Though now I was weakening—and freezing—very fast. My limp ex-captor weighed at least as much as I did, which necessarily slowed my pace. Yet I kept going, at right angles to our previous track, until I stumbled and fell headfirst into the snow. My face and hands were too numb to feel anything.

People were calling out on all sides, but none were in sight at the moment as the snow swirled down heavily. My fingers were like thick clubs as I pawed the man's hat from his head and put it on mine. It was almost impossible to open the closures on his suit but I managed it finally. Then plunged my arms inside, pushing my hands up into his armpits. They burned worse than the torture had, as feeling began to return.

Unconscious as he was, this chill clasp brought the gray man around. As soon as his eyes opened I pulled one hand out just long enough to make a fist and drive it into his jaw. He slept better then and I crouched there, half-covered with snow, until most of the pain had gone. One of the pursuers went by, very close, but never saw us. I felt no compunction in taking my captive's gloves, though I noticed he was stirring again as I pushed off through the snowdrifts.

After this I ran hard, panting but still going on. I was no longer cold and that was the only solace. When the rushing snowflakes began to thin I hurled myself backward into a snowbank, sinking well below the surface. There were still a lot of shouts, but they were weaker and in the distance now. I lay there until my breathing slowed down and I could feel the sweat freezing on my face. Only then did I roll over carefully and poke an opening in the side of the snow near my face.

There was no one in sight. I waited until the snow-fall started again, then ran on—full-tilt into a chain-metal fence. It vanished in the snow in both directions and rose up high above me. If it were wired for an alarm I had already tripped it so I might as well keep going. I clambered halfway up it, thought better of the idea—then dropped back into the soft snow below.

If an alarm had gone off they would be converging on this spot. I was not going to make it easy for them. Instead of going over at this place I hurried along the fence, running as fast as I could for what I hoped was at least ten minutes. I saw no one. Then I climbed the fence, dropped over it, and headed into the white wilderness. Running until I dropped. Then lay, half-buried in the snow until I got my wind back, before taking a cautious look in all directions.

Nothing. Just snow. No footsteps or marks of any kind. No bushes, trees, rocks or signs of life. A sterile white waste that went on and on for as far as I could see, delimitated only by the snow flurries on the horizon. One of them opened for a bit and I had a glimpse of the dark construction I had done all this to avoid.

I turned my back on it and shambled off into the driving blizzard.

TWELVE

"You're a free man, Jim, free. Free as the birds!"

I talked to myself in an effort at morale boosting and it helped a little bit. But there were no birds here to be free as. Nothing in the frozen waste except myself, slogging along one snow-impeded step after another. What had Kraj said about this planet, so many years ago? Doing a little memory-racking helped take my thoughts away from the present predicament for a few moments. All the memory training courses I had taken should be of some use now. I made the correct sequence of associations—and up the memory popped. Very good.

Always cold, he had said. True enough, as well as nothing green, nothing ever growing. This could be a midsummer day for all I knew. If so they could keep the winter. Fish in the sea, Kraj had said, all native life in the sea. Nothing lived on the snow. Except me, that is. And how long I lived depended on how long I kept moving. The clothes I was wearing were fine—as long as I put a little heat into them by putting one foot after the other. This could not go on forever. But I had seen one building when we landed. There should be others. There had to be something other than the unending snow.

There was—and I almost fell into it. As I put my foot down I felt something give way, shift out from under me. Purely by reflex I threw myself backward, falling into the snow. Before me the packed snow cracked open, moved away, and I looked down at the dark water. As the crack widened and I saw the edge of the ice I realized I was not on the land at all—but had walked out onto the frozen surface of the sea.

At this temperature if I fell in, as much as got a hand or foot wet, I would be dead. Frozen. I did not think much of this idea at all. Without standing up, keeping my weight spread out as much as I could, I pushed and slithered back from the brink. Only when I was well away from the edge did I dare stand and shamble back the way I had come, retracing the track of my rapidly disappearing footsteps.

"Now what, Jim? Think fast. There's water out there, which is very difficult stuff to walk on."

I stopped and looked around carefully in a complete circle. The snow had stopped falling, but the wind kept picking it up and whipping it about in gusty clouds. But, now that I knew what to look for, I could see the dark line of the ocean in the moments when visibility cleared. It stretched as far as I could see to right and left, directly across the route I had been taking.

"Then you won't go that way." I turned about. "From the looks of your ragged trail, mighty arctic explorer, you came in from that direction. There is no point in going back. Yet. The reception party will be sharpening their knives now. So think."

I thought. If the land were as barren as Kraj had said, their settlements and buildings would never be far from the ocean's edge. Therefore I had to stay close to the shore as I could without falling in. Follow the edge of the ice away from the direction I had come. Hoping that the spaceport building I had left was not the last one on the outskirts of town. I plodded on. Trying very hard to ignore the fact that the feeble glow of the sun was lower in the sky. When night fell so would I. I had no idea how long the days and nights on Kekkonshiki were—but I had a sinking sensation that, short or long, I would not be around to see the dawn. Shelter must be found. Go back? Not yet. Madness probably—but press on.

As the sun sank so did my hopes. The snow plain was darker now, but still featureless. Pushing through the heavy snow had wearied me to exhaustion and past. Only the knowledge that I would be dead if I stopped kept me putting one leaden foot in front of the other. Although I had pulled the hat far down over my face there was little sensation left in my nose and cheeks.

Then I found myself falling and had to stop. On my hands and knees in the snow, panting hoarsely, gasping for breath.

"Why not stay here, Jim?" I asked myself. "It will be easier than going on, and they say it is painless to freeze to death." It sounded like a good idea.

"It does not sound like a good idea, you idiot. Stand up and keep going."

I did, though it took a decided effort to struggle to my feet. An even greater effort to put one foot in front of the other. The simple act of walking took so much of my attention that the dark spots on the horizon were visible for some time before I became consciously aware of them. At first all I did was stand and stare, trying to gather my ice-numbed thoughts. They were moving, getting larger. With this realization I dropped full length in the snow. Lay there, watching intently, while three figures whipped silently by on skis no more than a hundred meters away.

After they had passed I forced myself to wait until they were out of sight before getting to my feet again. This time I was not even aware that it took any effort to do this. A small spark of hope had not only been kindled but burst into flame. The snow had stopped falling and the wind had died down. The tracks of the skis were sharp and clear. They were going someplace —someplace they had planned to be before dark. Well, so was I! Filled with sudden false energy I stepped onto the tracks and turned to follow them.

Although the energy burned away very quickly I still kept going. Now the approaching night brought encouragement instead of despair. The skiers were faster than I—but not that fast. They would be at their destination before nightfall and, hopefully, so would I. I slogged on.

The theory had to be correct, but in practice it was just not working out. The sun was still above the horizon, but behind thick and nasty-looking clouds, while the visibility was falling. The tracks were getting harder and harder to follow. And I had to rest. Tottering to a stop I looked up and blinked and peered ahead and saw a black smudge on the horizon. My brain was still in the deepfreeze and it took a good number of seconds to understand the significance of what I was looking at.

"Black is beautiful!" My voice was hoarse, almost gone. "It is not white snow and anything but snow is what you need right now."

My shambling walk became a far superior shamble, and I swung my arms and kept my head high. I tried to whistle too, but my lips were too cracked and cold for that. It was a good thing, since the wind had died as sunset approached and everything was deathly still. The dark blur resolved itself into a building—no, a group of buildings. Closer and closer. Dark stone. Small windows. Slanted roofs that would not collect snow. Solid and ugly. What was that squeaking, crunching sound, growing louder?

I was walking silently because I was still in the heavy snow. But those were footsteps on packed snow.

Getting closer. Back? No, drop. As I dived for cover the footsteps turned the corner of the nearest building.

About all I could do was lie there motionless and hope that I would not be seen. It was sheer luck that I was not. The footsteps, more than one person, grew louder and louder, crunched by and died away. I risked a quick look and saw the retreating backs of a column of short figures. About twenty of them. They turned another corner and were out of sight and hearing. With a desperate effort I scratched and scrambled to my feet and stumbled after them. Turning the corner behind the column just in time to see the last one vanishing into a building. A large and heavy door closed with a positive sound. That was for me. I was falling forward more than running, using my last reserves of energy, reserves I had not known I had. Ending up against the gray metal door, tugging at the handle.

It did not move.

Life has moments like this that are best forgotten and glossed over. In later years they may seem funny, and people can laugh over them when they are described after dinner, warming drink in hand, sitting by a roaring fire. At the time, though, this not only didn't seem funny, it seemed to be the absolute end.

Pulling didn't work and the handle did not turn when I fumbled at it with numb fingers. In the end I fell forward with exhaustion, leaning against the handle so I wouldn't fall. It pushed in and the door opened.

Just for once I made no attempt to reconnoiter what was on the other side. I half walked, half fell into the dark alcove inside and let the door close behind me. Warmth, delicious warmth washed over me and I just leaned against the wall and appreciated it. Looking down a long and badly illuminated corridor of roughly carved stone. I was alone, but there were doors all along the corridor and someone could emerge at any moment. But there was absolutely nothing I could do about it. If the wall had been taken away I would have fallen down. So I leaned there like a frozen statue, dripping melting snow onto the flagstones on the floor, feeling life ooze back as the heat seeped in.

The nearest door, just two meters before me, opened and a man stepped out.

All he had to do was turn his head a bit to spot me. I could see him clearly, even in the dim light, the gray clothes, long greasy hair—even the flecking of dandruff on his shoulders. He closed the door, still with his back turned, inserted a key and locked it.

Then he walked away from me down the corridor and was gone.

"It's almost time you stopped leaning here and thought of something to do, you rusty stainless steel rat," I encouraged myself in a throaty whisper. "Don't stretch your luck. Get out of the corridor. Why not through that door? After he locked it that way the chances are good that no one else is inside."

Good thinking, Jim. Except what do I do for a picklock? Improvise, that's what. I pulled off the gloves and tucked them into my jacket along with the fur hat. Though it was probably chill and dank inside the building it felt like a furnace after the outside. Life, as well as a certain amount of tingling pain, was coming back to my blue fingers. I took up the dangling end of the cable that hung from the metal collar still locked around my neck. Wires inside. Small but possible. I chewed them into a pointed mass with my teeth, then probed the lock.

It was a simple lock, the keyhole was very big, I have great burglar's skills. Well . . . I was lucky. I pushed and twisted and grunted and did everything but kick the door until the lock sprung open. Darkness beyond. I eased through, closed and locked it behind me—and breathed a very deep sigh of relief. For the first time since I had made my break I felt that I had a chance. With a happy sigh I slumped to the floor and fell asleep.

Well, almost. Tired and exhausted as I was, even as my eyes were closing, I realized that this was definitely not the right thing to do. To have come this far —and to be recaptured because I fell asleep. That was ludicrous.

"To work," I told myself, then bit my tongue. It worked fine. I lurched to my feet, muttering uncouthly at the pain, and felt my way through the blackness with outstretched hands. I was in a narrow room or corridor, little wider than my shoulders. There was nothing to be accomplished standing there so I shuffled forward to a bend where there was a dim glow of light. Still wary, I poked my head around it carefully to see a window set into the wall beyond. A small boy was standing on the other side of the window, looking directly at me.

It was too late to pull back. I tried smiling at him, then frowning, but he did not respond. Then he raised his fingers and ran them through his hair, patting the hair into place afterward. A bell rang dimly in the distance and he turned his head to look, then walked away.

Of course. One-way glass. A mirror from his side, a foggy window from mine. Set there with a purpose. To observe without being observed. To observe what? I walked around and looked at what was obviously a classroom. The boy, along with a number of counterparts, now sat at a desk watching the teacher intently. This individual, a gray man with equally gray hair, stood before the glass lecturing unemotionally. His face was expressionless as he talked. And so were—I realized suddenly—the faces of the boys. No smiling, laughter, gum-chewing. Nothing but stolid attention. Very unschoolroomlike, at least in my experience. The framed poster behind the teacher's back carried the message. In large, black letters it read:

DO NOT SMILE

A second sign to one side of it continued the message.

DO NOT FROWN

Both admonitions were being grimly obeyed. What kind of a schoolroom was this? As my eyes grew accustomed to the darkness I saw a switch and a loudspeaker next to the glass; the function seemed obvious. I flicked the switch and the teacher's voice rolled over me in drab tones.

". . . Moral Philosophy. This course is a required course and every one of you will take it and stay with the course until you have a perfect grade. There are no failures. Moral Philosophy is what makes us great.

Moral Philosophy is what enables us to rule. You have read your history books, you know the Days of Kekkonshiki. You know how we were abandoned, how we died, how only the Thousand were left alive. When they were weak, they died. When they were afraid, they died. When they allowed emotion to rule reason, they died. All of you are here today because they lived. Moral Philosophy enabled them to live. It will enable you to live as well. To live and grow and to leave this world and bring our rule to the weaker and softer races. We are superior. We have that right. Now tell me. If you are weak?"

"We die." The boyish voices chanted in expressionless harmony.

"If you are afraid?"

"We die."

"If you allow emotion . . ."

I switched off the program, having the feeling that I had heard more than enough for the moment. It gave pause for thought. For all of the years that I had been pursuing and battling with the gray men I had never bothered to stop and think *why* they were what they were. I had just taken their nastiness for granted. The few words I had overheard told me that their brutality and intransience was no accident. Abandoned, that's what the teacher had said. For reasons lost in the depths of time a colony must have been established on this planet. For ore or minerals of some kind, possibly. It was so inhospitable, so far from the nearest settled worlds, that there had to have been a good reason to come here, to work to establish a settlement. Then the people here had been abandoned. Either for local reasons, or during the bad years of the Breakdown. Undoubtedly the colony had never been meant to be self-sustaining. But, once on its own, it had to be. The majority must have died; a handful lived. Lived—if it can be called that—by abandoning all human graces and emotions, lived by devoting their lives simply to the battle for existence. They had fought this implacably brutal planet and had won.

But they had lost a good deal of their humanity in doing this. They had become machines for survival and had brutalized themselves emotionally, crippled themselves. And passed on this disability as a strength to the future generations. Moral Philosophy. But moral only when it related to surviving on this savage planet. Most unmoral when it came to subjugating other people. Yet there was a horrible kind of correctness to it —at least from their point of view. The rest of mankind was weak and filled with unneeded emotions, smiling and frowning, wasting energy on frivolities. These people not only thought they were better—their training forced them to believe that they *were* better. That and the inculcated generations of hatred of the others who had abandoned them here made them into the perfect galaxy conquerors. On their terms they were helping all the planets they conquered. The weak should die; that was right. The survivors would be led down the path of righteousness to a better life.

Being few in number they could not conquer directly but must work through others. They had engineered and managed the interplanetary invasions of the Cliaand. Invasions that had been succeeding until the Special Corps had busted things up. A busting-up that I had organized. No wonder they had been eager to get their cold little hands on me.

And this was the training ground. The school that made sure that every little Kekkonshiki kid was turned into an emotionless copy of his elders. No fun here. This school for survival that perverted every natural tendency of youth fascinated me. I was warm now, and safe enough for the moment, and the more I learned about this place the better chances I would have to make some plan to do something. Other than lurk in dark corridors. I went on to the next classroom. A workshop, applied science or engineering. Bigger boys here working on apparatus of some kind.

Some kind. *That* kind! I clutched the metal ring about my neck while I looked on, as hypnotized and paralyzed as a bird by a snake.

They were working on the little metal boxes with push buttons. Boxes with cables that ran to collars like the one I was wearing. Scientific torture machines. I moved my hand slowly and switched on the speaker.

". . . the difference is in application, not in theory. You assemble and test these synaptic generators in order to familiarize yourself with the circuitry. Then, when you go on to axion feeds you will have a working knowledge of the steps involved. Now, turn to the diagram on page thirty . . ."

Axion feeds. That was something I would have to learn more about. It was only a guess—but it seemed a sound one—that this gadget was the one I had never seen. But had experienced. The brain-stomper that had generated all my horrible memories. Memories of things that had never happened, never existed outside my brain. But which were none the better for that. It was all very revealing.

All very stupid of me. Standing there like a sadistic voyeur and not thinking of my flanks. Because of the teacher's voice muttering away and I did not hear the footsteps approaching, did not know the other man was there until he turned the corner and almost walked right into me.

THIRTEEN

Action is superior to thought in a situation like this and I hurled myself at him, hands grasping for his throat. Silence first then quickly unconscious. He did not move but he did speak.

"Welcome to Yurusareta School. James diGriz. I was hoping you would find your way here—"

His words shut off as my thumbs closed down on his windpipe. He made no move to resist nor did his expression change in the slightest as he looked me calmly in the eyes. His skin was loose and wrinkled and I realized suddenly that he was very, very old.

Although I am well equipped by training and circumstance to fight, and even kill, in self-defense, I am not really very good at throttling old grandfathers to death while they are quietly watching me. My fingers loosened of their own accord. I matched the man stare for stare and snarled in my most nasty manner.

"Shout for help and you are dead in an instant."

"That is the last thing I wish to do. My name is Hanasu and I have been looking forward to meeting you ever since you escaped. I have done my best to lead you here."

"Would you mind explaining that?" I let my hands fall, though I was still alert for trouble.

"Of course. As soon as I heard the radio report I tried to put myself in your place. If you went south or east you would end up among the buildings of the city where you would be quickly found. If you did not do this your course would take you west in the direction of this school. Of course if you headed north you would come to the sea very quickly and would then still have to go west. Operating on this theory I changed today's schedules and decided that all of the boys needed more exercise. They are all hating me now because they missed hours of classroom study that will have to be made up tonight. But they all did a number of kilometers on skis. Their course, not by chance, took them first south then west, to return here in a large loop along the shore. This was designed so that if you did see any of them you would follow them here. Is that what you did?"

There was no point in lying. "Yes. Now what do you plan to do?"

"Do? Why, talk to you of course. You were not seen entering the building?"

"No."

"Better than I expected. I was sure I would have to axion-feed some people. You are very ingenious, I should have remembered that. Now, the other end of this observation gallery leads to my office. Shall we go there?"

"Why? You're going to turn me in?"

"No. I want to talk to you."

"I don't believe you."

"Naturally, you have no reason to. But you have little choice. Since you did not kill me at once I doubt if you will do it now. Follow me."

At that Hanasu turned and walked away. There was

little else I could do except trot after him. And stay close. Maybe I couldn't chop him down in the prime of his senile life, but I could certainly grab him and wrap him like a package if he tried to call in any alarms.

The gallery wound up and down by many other classes, and I had tantalizing glimpses of what they were doing. But no chance to stop. I was right behind him when he climbed a short flight of steps and reached for the door handle. I put my hand out and stopped him.

"What's in here?" I asked.

"My office, as I said."

"Is anyone in there?"

"I doubt it. They have no permission to enter when I am not there. But I can look—"

"I think I would prefer to do that myself."

Which I did, and he was right. I felt very much like a lizard as I searched the room trying to keep one eye on him and the other on the fixtures, both at the same time. A narrow window opening out onto blackness, shelves of books, a large desk, files, a few chairs. I waved him to the one furthest from the desk—where any buttons or alarms would not be located. He went quietly, sitting and folding his hands while I prowled a bit more. There was a jug of water and a glass on the sideboard and I suddenly realized how thirsty I was. I poured and glugged and managed to finish all of it. Then I dropped into the chair behind his desk, put my feet up on it.

"And you really want to help me?" I asked, in my most sceptical tone of voice.

"Yes, I do."

"For openers you might show me how to take this collar off my neck."

"Of course. You'll find a key in the right hand drawer of the desk. The keyhole is just below the cable connection on the collar."

It took a bit of fumbling, but the collar finally snapped open and I threw it into the corner. "Great. A wonderful feeling." I looked around. "A nice office. Do you run this place?"

"I am the headmaster, yes. I was exiled here as punishment. They would have killed me, but they did not dare."

"I haven't the slightest idea what you are talking about. Would you care to explain?"

"Of course. The Committee of Ten rule this planet. I was on this committee for many years. I am an extremely good organizer. I originated and planned the entire Cliaand operation. When it was terminated, thanks to your efforts, I returned and became First of the Committee. That was when I attempted to alter our programs and they punished me for it. I have been at this school ever since. I cannot leave here nor can I change one word of the program which is fixed and immutable. It is a very safe prison."

This was getting more and more interesting. "What changes did you try to make?"

"Radical ones. I began to doubt all of our aims. I had been exposed to other cultures, corrupted they said, as I began to question ours more and more. But as soon as I tried to put my new ideas into force I was apprehended, removed, sent here. There can be no new ideas on Kekkonshiki . . ."

The door opened and a wheeled cart was pushed in by a small boy.

"I have brought your dinner, Headmaster," he said, then saw me behind the desk. His expression did not alter in the slightest. "That is the prisoner who escaped."

Only fatigue kept me in the chair; I had been through a lot this day and my mind was as tired as my body. What was I to do with this child?

"You are correct, Yoru," Hanasu said. "Come in and watch him while I go for help."

I was on my feet when I heard that, ready to knock some heads together. But Hanasu did not leave the room. Instead he stepped behind Yoru and silently closed the door. Then he took a black metal device from a shelf and touched it lightly to the back of the boy's neck. The boy froze, eyes open, immobile.

"There is no danger now," Hanasu said. "I will remove a few minutes of the lad's memory, that is all."

My throat closed and I felt the disgust—mixed with hatred and, yes, fear—rising within me. "That thing in your hand. What is it"

"The axion feed. You will have seen it many times, though of course you have no memory of that. It can remove memories and replace them with others. Now if you will step behind the door to the gallery the boy will enter again and leave."

Did I have a choice? I don't know. Perhaps the sight of the brain-tramping machine along with my fatigue was making me simple. I did not question; I just obeyed. Though I did leave the door open a crack to watch. Hanasu made some adjustments on the machine and pressed it to the boy's neck again. Nothing appeared to happen. Then he opened the door and regained his seat. A few seconds later the boy moved, pushing the cart further into the room.

"I have brought your dinner, Headmaster," he said.

"Leave it and do not return tonight. I do not wish to be disturbed."

"Yes, Headmaster." He turned and left and I emerged from my hiding place.

"That machine—it's the one they used on me?" I asked.

"Yes."

"It's the foulest, most disgusting thing I have ever heard of."

"It is just a machine," he said emotionlessly, then replaced it on the shelf. "I do not need food now and you will be hungry after your exposure. Help yourself."

Too many things had been happening too quickly for me to think about my appetite. But now that he had mentioned it I realized that I was hungry enough to eat a cow, raw. I threw back the cover on the plate and there was a rush of saliva at the sight of the food. It was the same tasteless dried fish ration I had had on the spacer, but was the finest dinner imaginable at that moment. I shoveled and chomped and listened to Hanasu.

"I am trying to understand your reasons for saying that the machine is disgusting. You mean the uses it is put to, don't you?" I nodded, my mouth too full to talk. "I can understand your reasoning. That is my trouble. I am very intelligent or I would not have been first in my classes and then first on the Committee. During the years I have given this much thought and have concluded that most of the people on this planet are both stupid and unimaginative. Intelligence and imagination are handicaps to basic survival in an environment as harsh as ours. We have selectively bred them out. Which means I am a sport, a mutant. These differences lay dormant during my early years. I believed everything I was taught and excelled in my studies. I did not question then because questioning is unknown here. Obedience is all. Now I question. We are not superior to all of the rest of mankind—just different. Our attempts to destroy or rule them all were wrong. Our liaison with the aliens to war on our own specie the biggest crime of all."

"You're right," I said, swallowing the last bite regretfully. I could have started all over again. Hanasu went on as though he had not heard me.

"When I discovered these facts I tried to change our aims. But it is impossible. I cannot even change one word of the training these children get—and I am in charge of the school."

"I can change everything," I told him.

"Of course," he said, turning to face me. Then his immobile face cracked, the corners of his mouth turned up. He smiled, ever so slightly—but it was still a smile. "Why do you think I wanted to get you here? You can do what I have labored my lifetime to accomplish. Save the people of this chill planet from themselves."

"One message would do it. Just the location of this planet."

"And then—your League would come and destroy us. It is tragic but inevitable."

"No. Wouldn't harm a hair of your heads."

"That is a jest and I do not like it! Do not mock me!" There was almost a trace of anger in his voice.

"It's the truth. You just don't know how a civilized society will react. I admit that a lot of people, if they knew who you were, would relish dropping a planet buster onto you. But with luck the general public will never know. The League will just keep an eye on your people to see that they don't cause any more trouble. And offer you the usual aid and assistance."

He was baffled. "I don't understand. They must kill us—"

"Stop with the killing already. That's your trouble. Live or die. Kill or be killed. That philosophy belongs to a darker stage of mankind's development that we have hopefully left behind. We may not have the best of all possible ethical systems or civilizations, but we at least have one that forbears violence as an institution. Why do you think your alien friends are doing so well? We no longer have armies or fleets to fight wars. We no longer have wars. Until people like yours come along and try to turn the clock back twenty thousand years or so. There is no need for killing as a tool of government. Ever."

"There must be the rule of law. If a man kills he be killed in return."

"Nonsense. That does not bring the dead back to life. And the society doing the killing then becomes no more than a murderer itself. And I see your mouth open for the next argument. Capital punishment is no deterrent to others, that has been proven. Violence breeds violence, killing breeds killing."

Hanasu paced back and forth the length of the room, trying to understand these—to him—alien concepts. I scraped the plate again and licked off the spoon. He sighed and dropped back into his chair.

"These things you tell me—they are beyond understanding. I must study them, but that is not important now. What is important is that I have made my mind up. I have been thinking about it for years and have decided. The Kekkonshiki plans must be stopped. There has been too much killing. It is only fit that it end by all of us being killed. You have told me this will not happen and I would like to believe you. But it does not matter. The message must be sent to your League."

"How?"

"You must tell me. Don't you think I would have

contacted them well before this if I had the means?"

"Yes, of course." Now I was pacing the floor. "No mail service to other planets, of course. No psimen here—or are there? Not that it's important. They wouldn't send *this* message. Radio?"

"The nearest League base is 430 light years away."

"Yes, well, we don't want to wait that long. I'll just have to find a way to get aboard one of the ships when they leave."

"I think that will be next to impossible."

"I'm sure of it. So what do you suggest. I know—you just asked me that same question. But there has to be a way. Maybe I had better sleep on it. Is there any place safe . . ."

I was interrupted by a high warbling sound. My eyebrows shot up.

"It is the communicator. An outside call. Stand against that wall where you will be out of range of the eye."

He seated himself at the desk and switched on.

"Hanasu," he said, face and voice frozen.

"A squad will reach you in a few minutes. They will seal all exits from the school. The foreigner has been traced in your direction and may be hiding there. Transportation is on the way now with six more squads. The school will be searched and he will be found."

FOURTEEN

"What evidence do you have that he is at the school?" Hanasu asked.

"Footprints in the snow. Going in your direction. He is either hidden in your school or he is dead."

"The students will aid in the search. They know the school buildings well."

"Issue that order."

Hanasu turned off the communicator and looked at me coldly. "We will not be able to carry out our plans after all. After they capture you they will use the axion feed to uncover my part in this. Do you wish to commit suicide to protect me?"

All of this was delivered deadpan with no change in tone. Although the room was chill I felt small prickles of sweat breaking out.

"Not so fast! All is not lost yet. Let us sort of save the suicide bit as a last resort. There must be some place I can hide?"

"No. They will look in every place."

"What about here? In your quarters. Tell them you searched and I'm not there."

"You do not understand our people. Whatever I— or anyone—might say the search will still go on as planned. We are very thorough."

"But unimaginative. I'll out-think them." I was feeling very unimaginative myself at the moment. Only the spurt of adrenaline generated by the suicide offer kept my engines chugging away at all. I looked around with a feeling of desperation. "The window! I can go through it, hide . . ."

"It does not open. It is fixed in place."

"Never opens? Not even in the summer?"

"It is summer."

"I was afraid you would say that. All is not lost yet!" There was a tinge of desperation in my voice because I had the awful feeling that everything was lost. "I know. If not inside I'll hide outside. There must be a way to get up onto the roof. Make repairs, nail down loose shingles."

"There are no shingles."

I resisted the urge to tear out a handful of hair. "Look—I don't mean it literally. But *is* there a way to get on the roof from inside the building?"

"There might be."

I fought hard with myself not to shake him by the neck until he gave me the right answers. "Are there plans? Blueprints of the school?"

"Yes. There in the file."

"Then get them. Quickly if you please." How long would it be before the search squads arrived? I cracked by knuckles and chewed my thumb and grabbed the sheets when he produced them. Flipping through them rapidly. Trying to ignore Hanasu's cheery observations.

"This is a waste of time. There is no escape. I do not wish to be interrogated with the axion feed. Therefore if you will not commit suicide I will . . ."

"Stop with the gloom already!" I snarled. It was depressing. My finger stabbed down. "There! What is that, that symbol?"

Hanasu held the sheet at arm's length, adjusted the light, squinted at it. My pulse rate doubled. "Yes, I see it," he finally said. "It is a door."

I clapped him on the back. "We're home free! If you do just as I say. First—order everyone in the school to get together. Not just the students but the teachers, cooks, gardeners, torture specialists. Everyone."

"We don't have any gardeners."

"I don't care!" My voice was beginning to crack and I had to fight a measure of control back into it. "Just get them all together—now—to help in the search. Talk first and I'll explain later."

He obeyed without question. Good old Kekkonshiki discipline. By the time he had made the announcement I knew what came next.

"I can't risk being seen, so you will have to get what I need from the labs. I want a power tool—make sure it's fully charged—at least ten long nails or screws, fifty meters of 500-kilo test line, a battery light and a lubricator. Where is the safest place for me to wait while you get them?"

"Here. There will be people in the corridors. By the time I return they will all be in the assembly hall."

"That was sort of my idea too."

"I do not know what you are planning but I will help you. There will be time for me to commit suicide after you are captured."

"That's it, Hanasu boy, always look on the bright side. Now go!"

He went and I prowled the carpet and looked for an unchewed fingernail to chew. I jumped when the communicator buzzed, but I stayed far away from it. Hanasu was gone all of four minutes. It felt like four days.

"They are all assembled and the search squads are here," he said.

"That's good news. Go down and organize them. See that they do a good and thorough job and work upward from the bottom to the top. I'll need all the time I can get since I have no idea what I will find."

"You are going on to the roof?"

"What you don't know you can't tell. Get moving."

"You are of course correct." He started for the door and, as he opened it, turned back for an instant. "Good luck. Isn't that what is said in a circumstance like this?"

"It is. Thanks. Good luck yourself. And I'll see if we can't avoid the mutual suicide pact."

I was out right behind him, running up the stairs as he tottered down, the construction diagram clutched in my hand. The climb was nice and warming, but I was panting loudly by the time I had reached the top floor. It had been a long day. Down to the end of the corridor to what appeared to be a storeroom. The door of which was locked.

"Jim diGriz laughs at locks," I laughed as I used one of the large nails to pick the even larger lock. The door swung open with a loud squeaking and I was through and slammed it behind me. There was no light switch that I could find and the air was frigid and musty. I turned on the light I had brought and looked around, treading between the heaped boxes and ancient files. The door I was looking for was at the far end of the room, a good four meters above the floor. There was no ladder.

"Better and better," I chortled and began to collect boxes that I could climb up on.

This took some time since I could not drag any of them and leave marks that might be noticed. I had to carry each one and stack it on the ones below to build a pile. Before I was done I was no longer feeling chill. In fact I sweated a bit when I thought of the searchers and wondered how close they were getting. I stacked faster.

The door was more of a trapdoor, a meter-square lid let into the angle of the roof just below the peak.

When I pushed at it it squeaked and a fine rain of rust particles showered down on me, which is about what I expected. I carefully applied the lubricant so it didn't drip, then wiped up all the rust. It would have been obvious it had been opened recently if I left it in its original condition. Now it was just another smooth-working trapdoor—and I only hoped that whoever was in charge of trapdoors like this wasn't around when the search was made. This was a chance I had to take. Now, when I pushed up on the trapdoor, it lifted easily and a blast of freezing air rushed in. I opened it all the way and poked my head out into the freezing night. Stars sparkled in the darkness above giving just enough light for me to see that there was absolutely no place of concealment on the roof.

"Solve that one when you come to it, Jim," I told myself with false good humor. "One step at the time, you crafty devil. You've licked them so far—you'll win in the end."

While I babbled this fatuous morale boosting I was driving a heavy nail into the coping outside. When it was well home I tied the end of the line to it. The 500-kilo test had enough diameter to take a grip, which is why I had selected it.

After that it was simply a matter of putting the boxes back where I had found them while trying not to think of the searchers getting closer every second. I was almost there—though I still wasn't quite sure where "there" was. All I wanted to do was to rush up to the roof and to close the trapdoor. What I did was to carefully go over the entire floor with my light to be sure I had left no traces of my passage. I found a lovely big footprint in the dust of one of the boxes; I turned the box on its side. Only when I was sure that nothing obvious indicated my visit did I go to the line leading up to the opening. After making sure that all my equipment was secure, I turned off the light, stowed it in my pocket and seized the line.

Behind me, in the darkness, I heard a key rattle in the lock.

Now, I don't know if there is any athletic event called the four-meter rope climb. But if there is I am sure that I set a new record at that moment. Without pausing for breath I was up it, hand over hand, grappling with insane desperation. One instant I was on the floor, the next I had the edge of the opening in my hand, was up and through it, stretched full length on the peak of the roof with one leg on each side, pulling up the rest of the rope. It seemed endless and I had finally pulled it all clear and was closing the trapdoor— when a light appeared in the room below.

"You take that side, Bukai, and I'll do this one," a gruff and toneless voice said. "Look behind all the boxes. Open ones big enough for a man."

With desperate caution I closed the door, holding fast with my fingertips until it was in place. What next? Would the searchers come up here? To ask the question was to have the answer. Of course they would. They would look everywhere a man could possibly be. Then I must find an impossible place. The featureless, welded metal surface on the roof filled me with no enthusiasm. It slanted away on both sides at a steep angle. Ahead of me, not five meters away, was the end of the roof. Featureless. Nothing in that direction, so perhaps in the other. I grunted as I pulled one leg up to turn around. It was then that I discovered that the metal was covered with a thin sheet of ice. My feet shot out from under me and I started to slide.

Down the slippery surface, my fingers scrabbling for holds that did not exist, faster and faster toward the edge and the drop to the frozen surface far below.

Until I remembered that the line was still attached. I grabbed at it with both hands. It slithered through my gloves. Then I gripped harder and held on. The shock on my arms when I stopped was something else again.

All I could do was hold on. Waiting for the pain to go away. Aware that my feet were hanging over the abyss. As soon as I could I dragged myself up, hand over hand, to the peak of the roof again. Where I remembered the searchers below and the fact that the trapdoor was going to be open very soon.

Of course the roof in the other direction was as featureless. Maybe they would not see me in the starlight.

I had to get as far away from the trapdoor as I could. Unfastening the rope with numb fingers, I straddled the peak and began to crawl along it, arms and legs widespread. Dragging myself really, sliding on the ice. Knowing that if I slipped to one side or the other that would be the end.

The end. That's what the roof did. Stopped. When I looked over my shoulder I saw that the trapdoor was clearly visible. As I would be to anyone putting his head out.

The line had held me before; it was going to have to do it again. Carefully and slowly, so I wouldn't lose my balance, I worked the power tool out and fitted one of the nails into the jaws. I would have to take the risk that the thick roof would muffle the sound. One touch on the trigger drove the nail in, through the metal, at the peak of the roof at the very end. My fingers were cold—and clumsy in the gloves—as I worked desperately to tie a knot on the line, to slip it over the nail, to tie a loop further down. To fit my foot into it and to let myself slide carefully over the edge. To hang down the end of the building. To ignore the creaking as the nail took up the strain.

There was a loud bang further back on the roof as the trapdoor was thrown open. I hung quietly, listening, smiling at my success as I heard the searchers talking clearly.

"See anything, Bukai?"

"No."

"Anyone on the roof?"

"No. Shall I come back inside?"

Well done, diGriz. The enemy outwitted again, you clever devil.

"No. Walk along the roof and look."

They were machines, not men. Any intelligent man would not have ventured out on that icy roof. He would have known better.

Any intelligent man would not have found me. These machine-minded morons just followed instructions until they succeeded.

The slitherings and gruntings grew closer and closer —and my rope twitched as someone pulled at it.

I looked up into the expressionless features of the searcher as he leaned over the end of the roof.

FIFTEEN

This was it. My eyes were adjusted to the starlight so that I saw his head jerk when he spotted me. Saw him sit up and turn his head about and open his mouth to shout.

"Ahiru."

Then he slipped. And for the first time I saw expression on the face of a gray man. Horror. He grabbed for the nail holding the rope. And missed. His fingers slapped hard on the roof. Then he slid away. Faster and faster. I could hear the sound of his sliding, but he made no other sound. Nothing. Then he was gone and I covered my ears because I did not want to listen to what happened below.

What next? The chill seeped into my bones as I hung there in the night and waited. There were muffled voices inside the building. I couldn't make out the words, then someone else joined the other man in the open trapdoor.

"Did Bukai say anything?"

"He spoke my name."

"As he slipped and fell?"

"Yes."

"That is not good."

"It is not. He is better dead. A man who shows emotion like that." Then the trapdoor closed.

What nice people. Bukai sure had friends. I suppose I felt sorrier for him than they did. Moral Philosophy! Before my fingers froze completely I pulled myself back up the rope and took a careful look. Trapdoor closed, roof empty. Back onto the peak and a slow and careful slither back. This was no time to slip and join the much-mourned Bukai.

After that I waited a long and frigid ten minutes, counting the seconds, until I was sure the room below would be empty. Or hoped it would be. The chill of the cold metal was biting through my insulated suit before I let myself pull at the door. My teeth chattering so hard I was sure they could hear them on the ground below. The room below was dark; they were gone.

There is a limit to the amount of stress a body can take and mine must have felt that it had had more than enough for the night. So when I rested on the floor for a bit while I thought about what to do next I instantly fell soundly asleep. So soundly that when I woke up, an unmeasurable amount of time later, I had no idea how long I had been sleeping. A minute or a day; there was no way to tell. What if everyone was awake? I would be trapped in here until nightfall. But how long were the days? I muttered curses at myself for falling asleep as I picked the lock as silently as I could. Opening the door with slow patience. The hall was empty. And the window across from the door was still black with night.

"Lucked out again, diGriz. Or maybe your subconscious timer is doing a better job than your conscious mind. Back to work."

The sleep had refreshed me and I tiptoed through the building, senses alert. All the doors were closed and I assumed that students and staff were sleeping off the strenuous affairs of the day. There was a light on in the headmaster's office so I put my eye to the crack as I opened it. He was sitting in the chair, awake, waiting for me. I slid through and closed it behind me.

"It is you," he said, and I saw that he had a glass of water raised to his lips. He set it down carefully on the desk.

"If that's water I'll have some," I said, reaching for it. "It has been a thirsty night."

"It is poison," he said tonelessly as I picked it up. I put it right back down.

"Suicide?"

"Yes. If I had to. I had no idea who would walk through the door first."

"Then they're all gone?"

"Yes. They found nothing. One of them fell off the roof and was killed. Are you responsible for that?"

"Only indirectly. But I saw him fall."

"They assume now that you have frozen to death in the snow. In the morning they will search for your body. It will not be a very stringent search because there is also some thought that you may have gone into the ocean."

"I almost did. But now that this evening's exhausting adventures are over I think we ought to go back to the topic under discussion when all the fun began."

"Getting a message to the League."

"That's it. In the quieter moments tonight I have been giving it some thought. I have an idea that might just work. Are you tired?"

"Not particularly."

"Good. Then I want to work in the electronics lab tonight. Can I do that—undisturbed?"

"It can be arranged. What do you want to do?"

"Dial up the library and get a diagram for a warp-drive detector. I assume you have enough parts and supplies here for me to build one?"

"We have the unit itself in our supplies. It is part of the training."

"Even better. Let's get to the lab and get started and I will show you what I want to do."

With Hanasu doing the fetching and me doing the assembly my device soon took shape. When it was completed I stood it on the bench and stepped back to admire it. A metal tube a meter long, streamlined on the top, open at the bottom, with two metal vanes running the length of it.

"A work of art," I said.

"What is its function?" Hanasu asked, a realist to the end.

"It gets attached to one of your spacers—and that will be our next problem. If I place it carefully it will never be noticed because it is a duplicate of the standard flare ejector that all ships carry. Only this one doesn't have flares—it has these." I held out one of the carefully constructed cylinders of plastic. "Inside the plastic is a power source and a solid state radio transmitter. I have made ten of these radios, which should be enough. Here is what happens. Every time the ship reenters normal space its warpdrive will cut off. When this happens the receiver in the nose detects the fact —and it launches one of the radios. There is a built-in time lag of a half an hour. More than enough time for the spacer to get on its way again. Then the radio switches on and begins broadcasting a strong signal on the League emergency wavelength. The signal contains my code identification and the location of this planet. And a call for help. Once the message gets through we simply sit back and wait for the space cavalry to arrive."

"Very ingenious. But what if there is no receiver nearby when the ship emerges from warpdrive?"

"I thought you might ask that. We're playing the law of averages. Most pilots use major navigation points most of the time. And most of these stars have a League station nearby. And most voyages make at least three downspace checks. One of the radio messages will have to be received."

"Hopefully. But it is better than nothing. Suicide is still possible."

"That's right. Always always look on the sunny side."

"How will you affix it to the spacer?"

"With an atomic welder." I held up my hand as he started to speak. "I know, no more funnies. That was a joke, chuckle-chuckle. I must find a way to get near one of the spacers unseen. It won't take more than a few minutes to do the job. Is the spacefield guarded?"

"There is a chainlink fence around it as you must know. And some guards at the gate. That is all I remember."

"Should be easy to get by that setup. Then I'll need your help with two things. I want to know when the next ship is leaving. And I'll need transportation to the spaceport."

"The information will be easy to supply. The earlier bulletin announced that the *Takai Cha* is going at 0645 hours today . . ."

"What time is it now?"

Hanasu blinked farsightedly at his watch and finally made out the numbers. "O-three-one-one," he said.

"Can you get transportation? Get me there in time?"

He had to think about this for a while before reluctantly nodding. "Normally, no. I have no reason to take the car out. But tonight I could report that I am volunteering for the search. They will probably say yes."

"We can only try."

The ploy worked. Within ten minutes we were bouncing over the iron-hard snow in an electrically powered, ski-mounted, propeller driven bone-breaker of an unsprung vehicle. No luxuries here. The heater was nonexistent, as were cushions on the seats. These people carried the hairshirt business entirely too far. My newly built radio-ejector was fitted with a strap so I could sling it over my shoulder. All the tools I might need were in a bag beside it. I looked out at the snowflakes whipping through the beams of the headlight and tried to plan ahead.

"How close can you get me to the fence?" I asked.

"As close as you like. There are no roads or marked tracks as you can see. The radio direction finder is followed from point to point."

"That's good news. Here is the plan. You drop me off at the fence and keep going. But mark the spot. Come back in exactly one hour. If you see any excitement or hear any alarms on the radio stay away."

"That is good. There will be enough time then for me to get back to the school and take the poison."

"Have it instead of breakfast, right. But don't do anything until you are sure they have me. There may be trouble, but they will not have an easy time grabbing hold of me."

"You have skied before?"

"I'm a champion."

It was a piece of cake. Twice we saw the lights of other cars, but they kept their distance. There was a good deal of rushing about this night. Then we were among dark buildings, bouncing over the ruts and doing suicide slides around corners. Hanasu was a real cold-nerved hotrod driver. The fence appeared and we paralleled it. The lights of a gate were visible ahead, then suddenly blotted out by a swirl of snow.

"I bail out here," I shouted. "Look at your watch and keep moving."

I threw my gear out into the snow and dived after it. The car was moving even before I landed, the blast from the propeller enveloping me in a sudden blizzard. It was dark, cold, miserable—and perfect cover. I took a detector from the tool bag and cautiously approached the fence.

There was absolutely nothing to it. I could have neutralized the simple alarm and cut my way through that fence with one eye closed, standing on one leg with my right hand behind my back. In fact, since I have always felt that a little bit of the old personal braggadocio goes no harm, I closed my eye, stood on one leg, grabbed the back of my neck with my hand—and did the job that way. Only when the links had been cut did I use both hands, holding the opening wide with one and pushing my oddments through with the other. Then it was the work of a moment to close the links with the molecular welder, put on the skis and slide off into the darkness. Behind me my tracks were already filling in. The first part of the job was done.

There was no problem in finding the spacer. In the darkness of the spaceport the ship was lit up brighter than day. I slithered toward it, staying close to the darkened buildings until I was behind the last one and looking out across the pad.

What a lovely sight. Lights burned brightly on towers, hissing when the snow blew against them. Men and vehicles scurried about servicing the tall spire of the ship. And there, prominent on the tailfin, was the name *Takai Cha*. This was the ship; it would be leaving soon just as planned.

Only how was I ever going to get close enough to fix my gadget into place?

SIXTEEN

That was a problem that obviously had but one solution. I was not going to get near the ship dressed as I was. But I could go there and work on the hull unremarked if I looked like one of the servicemen. So —I had to put the grab on one of the servicemen.

It was easy enough to find a dark corner behind some bins to stow my gear. But the kidnapping proved a good deal harder. I prowled around the fringes of the lit area like a wolf around a campfire, but with little result. No one left, no one arrived. The laborers labored on with Kekkonshikian plod, slowly and carefully with no display of emotion. I was displaying enough for all of them. Hanasu's watch tripped through the seconds and minutes—and then the hour. I had missed my appointment. What was worse I had not done the job I had come for. In less than an hour more the spacer would be taking off and there was still no way of getting near it.

My patience was gone, I was frothing slightly, and thinking up and rejecting one suicidal plan after another, when one of the servicemen decided to leave. He climbed down from the service gantry and walked slowly through the accumulated snow toward one of the buildings. I had to zip around the back, slither on my belly past some lit windows, then dash to the front again. It worked because I was just in time to see him enter a door marked "Benjo" in large letters. I whisked in right behind him and saw what a benjo was.

Being a respecter of certain rights I restrained myself and let him finish his communion with the gods of the watercloset before I decked him. This also made sure that his fingers were busy with zips and buttons. He never knew what hit him. I knew, it was the edge of my hand. After that it was off with his coveralls, zip-zip with the wire on ankles and wrists, another bit around his head to hold the gag into place, then back into the john. I wired him to the plumbing and locked him into the cubicle. I could have left him out in the snow to freeze to death, but this went very much against my own moral philosophy that I had been preaching to Hanasu. I also happened to believe in it. All would go well as long as he wasn't discovered until after the spacer took off. Which would not be long now.

His coveralls were a tight fit but I doubted if anyone

would notice the difference. His safety helmet covered my head and, with the collar turned up, very little of me was visible. Now for the final step.

I felt very conspicuous marching out under the lights with the tube under one arm, the tool bag slung casually in the other. And I had to walk slow, slog along when I wanted to run. This was hard to do, but my only safety lay in looking normal. Slow and steady. No one looked up, no one seemed to care about anything except his own work. I still sighed deeply when I reached the cab of the mobile gantry and threw in my things. The controls were simple enough. Slowly and carefully I drove around the base of the ship, out of sight of any of the servicemen for the moment. But there might be men watching whom I could not see in the darkness so I still moved at the sluggish pace of the others. Onto the gantry with my equipment, then slowly up beside the fin to the top, the standard location of the flare ejector.

Of course there wasn't one there. This made little difference since I was now taking the place of one of the only people who might spot my addition. It had to go on and on it went. The molecular welder hummed happily and the metal of the holddown fins was joined irrevocably to the metal of the hull. It would not be visible from the ground in the still driving snow.

"Do the job, baby," I said, patting it affectionately. Then back down and a quick vanishing act.

This time I didn't risk the walk but drove the gantry away instead, parking it in the shadow of the nearest building. Ten minutes to go. A car rolled out with the crew who stamped stolidly aboard. The other cranes and platforms were pulling away as well and it was getting very close to takeoff time.

"Why is that gantry here?" a voice behind me asked.

"Remstma?" I said in a muffled voice, not turning my head. Footsteps approached.

"I can't hear you. Repeat."

"Can you hear this?" I said as he got close, whipping about and getting both hands around his neck. His eyes popped, then closed as I banged his skull against the metal frame of the door. With the fate of worlds hanging in the balance I was not gentle. While I was tying him up the spacer took off. It was perhaps the nicest sound I had ever heard.

"You've done it, Jim, done it again," I congratulated myself since there was no one around to do it for me. "Countless generations yet unborn will bless your name. Countless Kekkonshikians will curse it daily, which is just too bad. The evil era of the gray men is drawing to a close."

There was a dark doorway nearby into which I dragged the latest unconscious body. As I dropped him, not too gently, inside the archway I saw that there was a very large and complex lock on the door. Why? The sign next to it revealed the reason—and at the same moment gave me the idea about what I had to do next.

Armory—authorized personnel only. Locked and forbidding—and what a perfect place to hide out. But only after a little misdirection. Easily enough done. I found my skis, put them on, then slid close to the lighted pad and waited for someone to see me.

These were the dullest and most unobservant people I had ever met. I slithered back and forth for five minutes without being spotted. It was really getting very boring and I was tired as well. In the end I swooped within ten meters of two of them and actually had run into some metal drums before they noticed me. When they looked up I put my arm over my face, hunched over, shivered, stumbled, then shot away into the darkness. All that was missing was a white arrow pointing at my back. They didn't react, of course, but I at least hoped they would remember me and the direction I had gone. Which was straight back to the fence. This time I made a big enough hole to drive a tank through, and left it open as well. Picking up speed I slid off into the darkness, heading for the wide open spaces, leaving a clear trail. Using my light at the same time to see if I could find a way to confuse it. The opportunity came soon enough. A car was grinding along, almost paralleling my own course, so I slanted over to join it. The thing was much faster than I was and was well past when I slid into its tracks. But I didn't go too far this way, just far enough to show our tracks merging and cutting back and forth across each other's.

When this had been well established I planted my poles and did a reverse turn that would have had my instructors glowing with pride. Up, over and down into the track of the other car ski. Landing cleanly in its track. Then sliding off in the opposite direction, no poles to leave marks, just kicking along well past the point where our tracks had merged.

After this I just kept on until the snow was covering the cars' tracks. It would cover mine too—and probably the earlier tracks. But if they did follow and see them they would have a false lead. Me, I was heading back to the city and safety.

They weren't early risers on Kekkonshiki, I'll say that much for them. A few were out, I saw other figures slipping by on skis, but I don't think any of them saw me. Nor did there seem to be any alarm. I reached the edge of the buildings on the far side of the spaceport and there still didn't seem to be anything busy happening. What next? I didn't want to break back in until the chase had gone out the other side. There seemed to be no sign that this was happening as yet. A light in a window beckoned warmly and I slipped over and looked in. A kitchen. Stoves merrily aglow and the cook getting things ready. It looked too good to resist. It was even harder to resist when the round-bottomed and apparently epicene cook turned toward the window and proved to be a female of the species. I had not talked to a female Kekkonshiki yet and the opportunity was too good to resist. Angelina was always accusing me of going after other girls and I should at least give her some sound basis for her suspicions. Even though this visit would negate all of my efforts in false-trail laying and necessitate another effort at misdirection—I still could not resist the temptation. Thus has it been ever with man and maid down through the ages. I found the door, took off my skis, stood them in the snow next to it, and went in.

"Good morning," I said. "Looks like another cold day, doesn't it."

She turned to look at me in silence. Young, wide-eyed and not too unattractive in an unpainted, pastoral sort of way.

"You are the one they are looking for," she said, with just a hint of emotion creeping into her voice. "I must go and give the alarm."

"You will not give the alarm." I leaned forward, ready to stop her.

"Yes, master," she said, and turned back to her pots and pans.

Master! I mulled this a bit and realized that the Kekkonshiki must be the Male Chauvinist Pigs of all time. They treated each other with coldness, lack of emotion, conscious and unconscious cruelty. How must they treat the women! Like this. As chattels, slaves probably. If any of them had protested in the past they had probably been booted out into the snow. A race of docile servants is what the men must have wanted and, obviously, after centuries of breeding they had achieved this noble goal.

My mind was torn away from philosophical speculation by the rich smells from the pots on the stove. It had been far too long since I had eaten last and, after all the exercise, I realized that hunger was nibbling at my interior with sharp teeth. In the rush of events I had again forgotten about food. Now my stomach was making up for this neglect with warning rumbles and groaning sounds.

"What's cooking, my fair flower of Kekkonshiki?"

She kept her eyes lowered and pointed out cooking utensils one by one, slowly and carefully. "In here is boiling water. In here is fish stew. In here are fish dumplings. In here is seaweed sauce. In here . . ."

"That's fine. I've heard enough. I'll have a portion of each, except for the boiling water that is."

She ladled some metal bowls full and I tucked in with a curved bone spoon. It was pretty tasteless stuff but I was not complaining. I even managed to eat the entire amount a second time before slowing down. As I slurped and shoveled I watched her closely, but she made no attempt to escape or give a warning.

"My name is Jim," I said, burping with appreciation. "What's yours?"

"Kaeru."

"Fine meal, Kaeru. A little bit light on the seasoning, but that's not your fault—it's the cuisine of the land. Are you happy in this job?"

"I do not know that word, 'happy.'"

"I'll bet you don't. What kind of hours do you work here?"

"I do not understand what you mean. I get up, I work, I go to bed. All days are like this."

"No weekends or holidays either I am sure. This world dearly needs some changes and they are on the way." Kaeru turned back to her work. "This culture won't have to be busted. It will just fall apart. The historians will keep a record of it and then it will vanish and a touch of civilization will enter your lives. Look forward to a happy tomorrow, Kaeru."

"Tomorrow I will work like today."

"Not for too long, I hope." With a delicate pinky nail I probed for a bit of seaweed stuck in the interstices of my teeth. "What time do you serve breakfast?"

She looked up at the clock. "In a few minutes when the bell rings."

"Who eats it?"

"The men here. The soldiers."

I was off the chair before the last syllable dropped from her lips, pulling on my gloves. "The food has been great, but I'm afraid I have to be pushing on. Heading south, you know. Got to make some time before the sun comes up. I suppose you wouldn't complain too much if I tied you up?"

"Do with me what you will, master." Her eyes were lowered when she said it. For the first time in my life I was ashamed of being a male chauvinist pig. "It will be better someday soon, Kaeru, I promise you that. And if I ever get out of this with a whole skin I'll send you a relief parcel. Some dresses, lipstick, and a textbook on fem lib. Now—is there a storeroom here?"

She pointed it out and I kissed her on the forehead. She immediately started to take her clothes off and was surprised when I stopped her. I could readily imagine what romantic lovers the gray men were! One more crime to answer for. Kaeru made no protests at all when I ushered her into the storeroom and locked it from the outside. She would be discovered soon enough when breakfast was late. But all I needed was a few minutes' headstart.

After leaving I carried the skis until I came to an icy stretch where my prints did not show. Only then did I put them on and head off in the opposite direction, muddling my trail again when I crossed other ski tracks. There was a good deal more of this sort of thing before I found myself back at the spaceport and, once more, cutting my way through the fence. I could hear sounds of distant excitement, sirens going and engines starting up which seemed to indicate that my earlier visit had been discovered at last. And about time too; I had to stifle a yawn. And wasn't the sky beginning to get a bit lighter? The hour had come to retire. I resealed the fence and slogged on.

With very little effort I reached the armory unseen. The man I had left in the doorway was gone, as well as everyone else from the vicinity. The lock yielded to my attentions and I breezed through and sealed it behind me. Well done, Jim, you tricky devil. With leaden feet I toured the interior, finally finding a locked room of fragmentation grenades that should be untouched for a while. In and down behind them, hidden from the world, secure and gone to ground, I yielded at once to the lure of sleep.

It was wonderful. I felt that I could have slept forever. Except something was disturbing me. I swam back up to consciousness and saw that it was daylight. Was that what had woken me?

No, it was a key turning in the lock, the door creaking open.

I had only myself to blame. I had forgotten the plodding searchers in the school. These people could not be tricked by any kind of ruse. As soon as they knew I was still alive they simply started a search of every building in the city. The game was up.

SEVENTEEN

I was refreshed by the long sleep, my bloodstream was filled with rich fish protein—and I was very angry at myself for not making a better attempt at hiding out. But, like the rest of us, I would rather be angry at someone else rather than admit the fault was mine, so I instantly transferred my temper to the hapless man who came through the door, waiting until he came close, then springing upon him like a jungle animal. Then tripping over the skis which I had forgotten about and falling in a tumble at his feet. Not that this made much difference to the outcome since these people had no idea at all about infighting. It was the old twist and crunch once again. After which I shouldered the skis, stepped over the unconscious body, and peeked out of the door. More of them were searching the building, on all sides of me, as I plodded toward the exit. One of them glanced up and I actually did three paces more before he reacted.

"He is there, trying to escape," he said in a dull monotone.

"Doing it too!" I shouted and rushed through the door, right over the man coming in. Then it was just a matter of stepping into the skis and zipping away.

Of course this did no good at all, other than put off the inevitable for a few more minutes. The fence had been repaired, the entrances were guarded—and my tool kit was back in the armory. As I rushed around, wondering what to do next, I heard the car engines starting up. Grab one of them? Rush the gate. Then what? One man against an entire world wasn't going to do me much good on this planet. Maybe I could find another hiding place in the city.

Why? I couldn't escape these people. Why put off the inevitable? I stopped to think about this, then remembered what they could do with the axion feed and I started up again. Maybe Hanasu was right and suicide

was the only answer. But I rejected this out of hand;
I'm just not the suicide type, as I keep telling myself.

All of this kept me occupied. Rushing about the
spaceport with the pursuit hotting up behind me, having a good suffer over my approaching fate, racking my
depressed mind for a way out. With my attention wan-
dering like this I wasn't aware of the sound of the rocket until it was right overhead. Like everyone else on the
field I stopped and looked up and gaped.

Out of the low cloud it dropped, riding its flame to
the ground, a small scout ship.

With the joined rings of the League upon its flank.

"It worked!" I shrieked and went straight up in the
air. I landed on the move and made wow-wow sounds
with my hand over my mouth as I streaked for the
landing pad. The spacer was still bounding on its landing shocks when I came rocketing up. Needless to say
no one followed me since the locals were not as en-
thusiastic about this arrival as I was. When the hatch
ground open I stood below it.

"Welcome to Kekkonshiki," I said to the man who
emerged, squinting in the reflected glare. "Claim this
planet for the League, oh conqueror."

"I don't know anything about that," he said. A
young man with an awful lot of hair and beard, wearing a soiled and patched shipsuit. "I got a message to
pick up one James Bolivar diGriz."

"You are looking at him."

"So are the locals. Only they are coming this way
with a lot of guns. Get aboard."

"Not until I make it plain to these types just what
has happened."

I was happy to see a familiar face in front of the
pack. Kome, the commander and captain of the ship
who had brought me here. "Drop the gun," I told him.
He raised it instead.

"You will come with me. Both of you."

I saw red. These people were so dense it sickened
me. What they had done, the untold number dead because of their infernal plans, sickened me even more.

"Don't shoot, I beg of you!" I cried, hands in the
air, stumbling toward him. Kicking up hard on his

wrist so the gun went flying. I caught it, grabbed his arm, twisted him around and ground the gun into the side of his neck as hard as I could.

"Listen to me, you ice-cold idiots!" I shouted. "It's all over, finished, through. You have lost. You will cause no more trouble in the galaxy. Your only strength was secrecy, so you could work away like roaches inside the wall. But that's over now. Don't you see the insignia on this ship? It's a League ship. They *know* about you now. Know who you are and where you are. Justice has arrived in the shape of this handsome pilot who brings you his message of wrath and who announces that he has just conquered your planet."

"Have I?" the pilot gasped.

"Shut up, you dumbhead, and do your job."

"My job was to get you."

"You've been promoted. Take their guns."

There was a little edge of desperation in my voice because they were raising their guns. Knowing their attitudes I knew they would calmly shoot Kome in order to get me. I gave his arm an extra twist and pressed the muzzle of the gun deeper into his flesh.

"Come on, Kome, tell them to put their weapons away and surrender. If one shot is fired I'll see that you are all tortured to death with hot pokers."

Kome thought and thought in his plodding Kekkonshiki way. Then made his mind up.

"The presence of this ship might be an accident."

"No accident," the pilot said. "I'll show you the message I received. It went out with a general alarm ordering all ships in the area to this planet. We've been looking for you people for some time. I'll get the message."

"There is no need for the message. Kill them both," Kome ordered loudly. "If they lie it will be the end of them. If they do not lie it will make no difference for we are as dead."

"Move aside, Kome," the nearest man said, sighting his gun. "Or I must shoot you."

"Shoot me" was the toneless answer.

"Stop it!" I ordered, shooting the man in the arm so his gun went flying. "It's no use."

They thought otherwise. The guns were swinging about when the pilot delivered the message he had been talking about. Not the one they had been expecting. He wasn't too stupid; scout pilots rarely are.

The nose turret whipped about swiftly and explosive shells rained down on all sides. I wasted no time, rapping Kome on the skull with the gun so he would come along quietly, then adding a few shots of my own at the others to keep their heads down. Into the airlock and finger on closing button. Kome wasn't quite unconscious but a kick in the side of the head fixed that. Normally I am not vicious, but this time I enjoyed the sadistic pleasure.

"Get flat, this will be a 5G takeoff," the pilot said.

It was too, and I clunked the last centimeters to the deck and got a good slam on the back of my head. By the time I stopped seeing unusual colors the pressure eased and I floated up.

"Thanks," I said with all sincerity.

"A pleasure. Those were some nasty-looking friends you had down there."

"Those were the loonies who started this whole war. And, dare I ask, how is it going?"

"We're still losing it," he said with black gloom. "There is just nothing we can do."

"Don't say that, it's bad luck! And head for the nearest station with a psiman because I have some urgent business to transact. You wouldn't happen to know if a load of prisoners escaped from the aliens?"

"The admirals, you mean? They're back, and a sorry lot they are too. I mean, normally you don't care what happens to senior officers, like they're different life forms or something. But this was a not-too-nice thing."

"They'll be cured. Excuse me smiling but my wife and sons were responsible for that escape so it means they are safe."

"You got some family."

"You can say that again!"

"You got some family."

"Don't take me too literally, though I enjoy hearing it. Now will you please pour the juice to this thing and get us to the psiman. There is much to be done."

By the time we rocketed into the satellite station I had my messages all written. Something big with a lot of guns and a full complement of troopers would be spared from the war to bring civilization to the Kekkonshiki natives. There were exact instructions on how they were to find Hanasu and put him in charge of the pacification. Justice, revenge and everything else could come later. Right now it was important just to neutralize the gray men to guard our flank. The war still had to be won. I read all the reports in the ship and by the time I had reached the Special Corps Main Base I had a number of plans made. All of them were driven from my mind by the sight of the svelte figure of the woman I loved.

"Air . . ." I gasped after a number of minutes of close and passionate embrace. "It's nice to be home."

"There's more in store, but I assume you want to look after the war a bit first."

"If you don't mind, precious mine. Did you have any trouble admiral-saving?"

"None. You had everything in a lovely turmoil. The boys learn fast and are very good at this sort of job. They are also off now in the navy, doing important things. I worried about you."

"You had very good reason to—but it's all over now. You didn't, by chance, happen to pick up any souvenirs when you were passing through that alien treasury?"

"I left that to the twins, who take after their father. I'm sure they pinched a good bit for themselves, but what they passed on will make us independently wealthy for life. If we live."

"The war, of course." My elation turned to depression at the thought. "What is happening?"

"Nothing good. As you observed the aliens on their own are a little on the stupid side. Once the gray men were out of the picture leadership must have been divided. But there still must have been a few commanders left who were bright enough to come in out of the rain because they launched an all-out attack. Left their base completely. Just took everything they had and came after us. So we ran, and are still running. Just picking

away at their fringes to let them think we will stand and
fight. But we can't afford to. They outnumber us and
outgun us at least a thousand to one."

"How long can this last?"

"Not much longer, I'm afraid. We're almost past
all of our inhabited planets and will be coming out
soon in intergalactic space. After that we can retreat
no more. Or if we do the uglies will see what we are
doing and even they are smart enough to figure this
one out. All they have to do then is leave a small force
to keep us at bay, then they can turn and start attack-
ing our planetary bases."

"You don't make it sound too good."

"It isn't."

"Do not worry, my sweet." I clutched her and kissed
her a bit more. "But your own little Slippery Jim will
save the galaxy."

"Again. That's nice."

"I was ordered to come here," a familiar voice said.
"Just to see you kissing and hugging? Don't you know
there is a war on? I'm a busy man."

"Not as busy as you are going to be soon, Professor
Coypu."

"What do you mean?" He shouted angrily and
clashed his protruding molars in my direction.

"I mean you are about to make the weapon that will
save us all and your name will ring down through the
history books forever. Coypu, Galaxy Savior."

"You're mad."

"Don't you think you're the first one to ever say
that. All geniuses are called mad. Or worse. I read a
report highly secret that you now believe in parallel
universes . . ."

"Silence, you fool! No one was to know. Specially
you!"

"An accident, really. A safe just happened to fall
open when I was passing and the report dropped out. Is
it true?"

"True, true," he muttered tapping his fingernails on
his teeth unhappily. "I had the clue from your escapade
with the time helix when you were trapped in a loop of
time in a bit of past history that did not exist."

"It existed for me."

"Of course. Just what I said. Therefore, if one possible different past could exist, then an infinity of different pasts—and presents—must exist. That's logical."

"It certainly is," I cheered. "So you experimented."

"I did. I have gained access to parallel universes, made observations and notes. But how does this save the galaxy?"

"One more question first, if you please. Is it possible to pass through into these other universes?"

"Of course. How else could I have made my observations? I sent a small machine through to make readings, take photographs."

"How big a machine can you send through?"

"It depends on the power of the field."

"Fine. Then that is the answer."

"It may be an answer to you, Slippery Jim," Angelina said with some puzzlement, "but it doesn't make much sense to me."

"Ahh, but just think, lover mine, what can be done with a machine like that. You mount it on a battleship with plenty of power. The battleship joins our space fleet and the fighting begins with the enemy. Our forces flee, the battleship limps behind, the enemy rushes up, the field is turned on—"

"And every one of those awful creepy-crawlies and all of their guns and things zip right through into another universe and the menace is over forever!"

"I was thinking of something roughly like that," I said modestly, polishing my fingernails on my chest. "Can we do it, Coypu?"

"It is possible, possible . . ."

"Then let us get to your lab and look at the gadget and see if the possible can be turned into the tangible."

Coypu's newest invention did not look like very much at all. Just a lot of boxes, wires and assorted gadgetry spread all over the room. But he was proud of it.

"Still in rough shape, as you can see," he said. "Breadboarded components. I call it my parallelilizer . . ."

"I would hate to say that three times fast."

"Don't joke, diGriz! This invention will change the fate of the known universe and at least one unknown one."

"Don't be so touchy," I said soothingly. "Your genius will not go unmarked, Prof. Now, would you be so kind as to demonstrate how your parallelilizer works."

Coypu sniffed and muttered to himself while he made adjustments on the machine, threw switches and tapped dials. The usual thing. While he was busy I was busy too giving Angelina a quick hug and she hugged right back. The professor, wrapped up in his work, never noticed that we were wrapped up in ours. He lectured away while we snogged.

"Precision, that is the important thing. The various parallel universes are separated only by the probability factor which is very thin, as you can well imagine. To pick just one probability out of all the countless possible ones is the trickiest part of the operation. Of course the probabilities that vary the least from ours are the closest, while completely changed probability universes are the most distant and require the most power. So for this demonstration I will take the nearest one and open the portal to it, *so!*"

A last switch was thrown and the lights dimmed as the machine sucked in all the available power. On all sides machines hummed and sparkled and the sharp smell of ozone filled the air. I let go of Angelina and looked around carefully.

"You know, Professor," I said. "As far as I can see absolutely nothing has happened."

"You are a cretin! Look, there, through the field generator."

I looked at the big metal frame that was wrapped with copper wire and glowing warmly. I could still see nothing and I told Coypu so. He screeched in anger and tried to pull out some of his hair, failing in this since he was almost bald.

"Look through the field and you see the parallel universe on the other side."

"All I can see is the lab."

"Moron. That is not *this* laboratory, but the one on the other world. It exists there just as it does here."

"Wonderful," I said, smiling, not wanting to offend the old boy. Though I really thought he was crackers. "You mean if I wanted to I could just step through the screen and be in the other world?"

"Possibly. But you might also be dead. So far I have not attempted to pass living matter through the screen."

"Isn't it time you tried?" Angelina asked, clutching my arm. "Only with some living matter other than my husband."

Still muttering, Coypu exited and returned with a white mouse. Then he put the mouse in a clamp, fixed the clamp to a rod, then slowly pushed the mouse through the screen. Absolutely nothing appeared to happen other than that the wriggling mouse managed to squirm out of the clamp and drop to the floor. It scuttled aside and vanished.

"Where did it go?" I asked, blinking rapidly.

"It is in the parallel world, as I explained."

"The poor thing looked frightened," Angelina said. "But it didn't appear to be hurt in any way."

"Tests will have to be made," Coypu said. "More mice, microscopic examinations of tissue, spectroscopic determination of factors . . ."

"Normally yes, Prof," I said. "But this is war and we just don't have the time. There is one real time saver that will enable us to find out right now—"

"*No!*" Angelina called out, being faster on the uptake than the professor. But she said it too late.

Because even as she called out I was stepping through the screen.

EIGHTEEN

The only sensation I felt was sort of a mild tingle, though even this might have just been a product of my fevered imagination since I was expecting to feel something. I looked around and everything looked very much the same to me—though of course all of the parallelilizer equipment was missing.

"Jim diGriz, you come back at once—or I'll come after you," Angelina said.

"In just a moment. This is a momentous instant in the history of science and I want to experience it fully."

It was disconcerting to look back through the screen and find that the view of the other lab—as well as Angelina and the professor—vanished when I walked off to one side. From the front the field itself was invisible, though when I walked around behind it it was clearly visible as a black surface apparently floating in space. Out of the corner of my eye I saw something move; the mouse scuttling behind a cabinet. I hoped that he liked it here. Before returning I felt I had to mark the important moment some way. So I took out my stylus and wrote SLIPPERY JIM WAS HERE on the wall. Let them make of that what they will. At that moment the door started to open and I instantly nipped back through the screen. I had no desire to meet whoever was coming in. It might even be a parallel-world duplicate of me, which would be very disconcerting.

"Very interesting," I said. Angelina hugged me and Coypu turned off his machine. "How big can you make the screen?" I asked.

"There is no physical or theoretical limit on its size since it doesn't exist. Now I am using metal coils to contain the field, but they are dispensable in theory. Once I am able to project the field without material containment it will be big enough to send the entire alien fleet through."

"My thought exactly, Professor. So, back to your drawing board and get cracking. Meanwhile I'll break the news to our masters."

Calling together all of the chiefs of staff was not easy since they were deeply involved in running the war, if not in winning it. In the end I had to work through Inskipp who used the powers of the Special Corps to call the meeting. Since they were using this base as headquarters for defense they found it hard to ignore the call of their landlord. I was waiting when they arrived, crisp and shining in a new uniform, a number of real medals, and a few fakes, pinned to my chest. They grumbled to each other, lit large cigars and scowled in my direction. As soon as they were all seated I rapped for attention.

"Gentlemen, at the present time we are losing the war."

"We didn't have to come here to have you tell us that," Inskipp snarled. "What's up, diGriz?"

"I brought you here to tell you that the end of the war is now in sight. We win."

That caught their notice, all right. Every grizzled head was now leaning in my direction, every yellowed or drooping eye fixed upon me.

"This will be accomplished through the use of a new device called the parallelilizer. With its aid the enemy fleet will fly into a parallel universe and we will never see them again."

"What is this madman talking about?" an admiral grumbled.

"I am talking about a concept so novel that even my imaginative mind has difficulty grasping it, and I expect that your fossilized ones can't understand it at all. But try." A deep growl ran through the room with that, but at least I had their attention now. "The theory goes like this. We can time travel to the past, but we cannot change the past. Since we obviously make changes by going into the past, those changes are already part of the past of the present we are living in." A number of eyes turned glassy at this but I pressed on. "However if major changes are made in the past we end up with a different past for a different present. One we don't know about since we are not living in it, but one that is real for the people who do exist there. These alternate time lines, or parallel universes, were inaccessible until the invention of the parallelilizer by our Corps genius, Professor Coypu. This device enables us to step into other parallel universes, or to fly in or get there in a number of interesting ways. The most interesting will be the generation of a screen big enough for the entire alien fleet to fly through so they will never bother us again. Any questions?"

There certainly were, and after a half an hour of detailed explanations I think I had convinced them all that something nasty was going to happen to the aliens and the war would be over, and they certainly approved of that. There were smiles and nods, and even a few muffled cheers. When Inskipp spoke it was obvious that he spoke for them all.

"We can do it! End this terrible war! Send the enemy fleet into another universe!"

"That is perfectly correct," I said.

"IT IS FORBIDDEN," a deep voice, a disembodied voice, said. Speaking apparently from the empty air over the table.

It was very impressive and at least one officer clutched at his chest, whether for his heart or some religious tract was not clear. But Inskipp, con man himself, was not conned.

"Who said that? Which one of you is the joker with the ventriloquial projector?"

There were loud cries of innocence and much looking under the furniture. All of which stopped when the voice spoke again.

"*It is forbidden because it is immoral. We have spoken.*"

"*Who* have spoken?" Inskipp shouted.

"We are the Morality Corps."

This time the voice came from the open doorway, not out of the air, and it took an instant to realize this. One by one the heads snapped around and every eye was fixed on the man when he came in. And very impressive he was too. Tall, with long white hair and beard, wearing a floor-length white robe. But it was hard to impress Inskipp.

"You are under arrest," he said. "Call the guards to take him away. I've never even heard of the Morality Corps."

"Of course not," the man answered in deep tones. "We are too secret for that."

"You, secret," Inskipp sneered. "My Special Corps is so secret that most people think it is just a rumor."

"I know. That's not too secret. My Morality Corps is so secret there aren't even any rumors of its existence."

Inskipp was turning red and beginning to swell up. I stepped in quickly before he exploded. "That all sounds very interesting, but we will need a little proof, won't we?"

"Of course," he fixed me with a steely gaze. "What is your most secret code?"

"I should tell you?"

"Of course not. I'll tell you. It is the Vasarnap Cipher, is it not?"

"It might be," I equivocated.

"It is," he answered sternly. "Go then to the Top Secret computer terminal there and give it this message in that cipher. The message is 'Reveal all about the Morality Corps.'"

"I'll do that," Inskipp said. "The agent diGriz is not cleared for the Vasarnap Cipher." That's how much he knew. But all the eyes were upon him as he went to the computer terminal and rattled the keys. Then he took a cipher wheel from his pocket, plugged it into the terminal and typed in the message. The speaker scratched and the monotone voice of the computer droned out.

"Who makes this request?"

"I, Inskipp, head of the Special Corps."

"Then I will reveal that the Morality Corps is the top priority secret force in the League. Its orders must be obeyed. The orders will be issued by the Morality Corps top executive. At the present time the top executive is Jay Hovah."

"I am Jay Hovah," the newcomer said. "Therefore I repeat. It is forbidden to send the alien invaders into a parallel world."

"Why?" I asked. "You don't mind our blowing them up, do you?"

He fixed his stern gaze upon me. "To battle in self-defense is not immoral. This is the defense of one's home and loved ones."

"Well if you don't mind our blowing them up— what is the complaint about slipping them into another world line? That won't hurt them half as much."

"It won't hurt them at all. But you will be sending ravening aliens in a giant battle fleet into a parallel universe where they did not exist before. You will be responsible for their killing all the humans in that universe. That is immoral. A way must be found to eliminate the enemy without making others suffer."

"You can't stop us," one of the admirals shouted in anger.

"I can and I will," Jay Hovah said. "It says in the Constitution of the League of United Planets that no immoral acts will be indulged in by member planets or by forces operating under the orders of member planets. You will find that a clause is included in the original agreement signed by all planetary representatives that a Morality Corps will be founded to determine what is moral. We are the top authority. We say no. Find yourself another plan."

While Jay was talking all the little wheels in my head were spinning busily. They stopped finally and the winning numbers came up.

"Stop this bickering," I said, then had to repeat myself, shouting, before I was heard. "I have come up with the alternative plan." This quieted them down and even Jay stopped pontificating for a bit to listen. "The Morality Corps protests that it would be an immoral act to shoot all the nasties into a parallel universe where they can work their will upon the human beings there. Is that your argument, Jay?"

"Put rather crudely, but in essence, yes."

"Then you wouldn't protest at all if we pushed the enemy into a parallel universe where there were *no* human beings?"

He opened and shut his mouth a few times at that one, then scowled fiercely. I smiled and lit a cigar. The admirals buzzed, mostly with bafflement since they weren't too bright or they would have enlisted in the peacetime navy.

"I would like a second opinion," Jay Hovah finally said.

"By all means, but make it fast."

He glared at me, but pulled out a gold pendant that hung about his neck and whispered into it. Then listened. And nodded.

"It would not be immoral to send the aliens into a

universe where there were no human beings. I have spoken."

"What is happening?" a bewildered admiral asked.

"It's very simple," I told him. "There are millions, billions, probably an infinite number of parallel galaxies. Among this number there must surely be one where Homo sapiens never existed. There might even be a galaxy populated only by aliens where our enemies would be made welcome."

"You have just volunteered to find the right one," Inskipp ordered. "Get moving, diGriz, and find us the best place to send that battle fleet."

"He shall not go alone," Jay Hovah announced. "We have been watching this agent for a long time since he is the most immoral man in the Special Corps."

"Very flattering," I said.

"Therefore we do not take his word for anything. When he looks for the correct parallel galaxy one of our agents will accompany him."

"That's just fine," I told him. "But please don't forget that there is a war on and I don't want one of your leaden-footed, psalm-singing moralists hanging around my neck." Jay was whispering instructions into his communicator. "This is a military operation and I move fast . . ."

I shut up when she walked in the door. From Jay's outfit, if the long robe meant anything, but it was filled quite differently from his. Some very interesting curves revealed rather than concealed. Honey-blonde hair, rose lips, shining eyes. Very attractive package in every way.

"This is agent Incuba who will accompany you," Jay said.

"Well, in that case I withdraw my objections," I smarmed. "I'm sure she is a very efficient officer . . ."

"Oh, yes?" a voice spoke out from the thin air, the second time this day. Only this one was a female voice that I instantly recognized. *"If you think you are going galaxy-hopping alone with that sleazy sexpot, Jim diGriz, you are very mistaken. You had better book three tickets."*

NINETEEN

"What kind of secret war conference is this?" Inskipp howled. "Is everyone listening to it? That was your wife on the eavesdropping circuit, diGriz—wasn't it?"

"Sounded very much like her," I said a little too heartily. "I guess you ought to have the security arrangements checked out. But you'll have to take care of that yourself because I have to go look at some other galaxies and that is a time-consuming business. You'll get my report soonest, gentlemen."

I exited with Incuba a few steps behind me. Angelina was waiting in the corridor. Eyes glowing like a female lioness, fingernails hooked like claws. She seared my skin with one sizzling glare, then turned her destroying gaze on Incuba.

"Do you plan to wear that bathrobe for this arduous trip?" she asked, voice close to absolute zero. Incuba looked Angelina up and down, her expression unchanged although her nostrils flared ever so lightly as though she had sniffed something bad.

"Probably not. But whatever I wear it will certainly be more practical—and a good deal more attractive than *that*."

Before the warfare escalated I took the coward's way out and dropped a mini smoke-grenade. It banged and puffed and took their attention off their differences for an instant. I spoke quickly.

"Ladies, we leave in one half an hour so please be ready. I am off to the lab now to set things up with Professor Coypu and I hope that you will join me there."

Angelina joined me now, grabbing my arm with talons sunk deep, marching me off down the corridor, hissing words into my ear—then biting it for emphasis.

"One pass at that tramp, one look, one touch of your

131

hand on hers and you are a dead man, Dirty Old Jim diGriz."

"What happened to innocent-until-proven-guilty?" I groaned, rubbing the aching earlobe. "I love you and none other. Now, can we drop this and get on with the war. And get Coypu to set up our investigation."

"You have only one choice of a possible galaxy," Coypu said, after I had explained the situation.

"What do you mean?" I was shocked. "Billions, an infinite number you said."

"I did. That many exist. But we can get access for a large object, such as a spaceship, to only six. After that the energy demand is too great to open a screen more than two meters in diameter. You're not going to get many aliens through a hole that big."

"Well, that's at least six universes. So why do you say only one?"

"Because in the other five this laboratory exists and I have observed myself or other humans in it. In the sixth, which I call Space Six, there is no laboratory or Corps base. The screen opens into interstellar space."

"Then that is the one we must try," a golden voice said, and Incuba tripped in through the door. She was fetchingly garbed in tight shipsuit, kinky black boots and other interesting things that I knew better than to notice since Angelina was right behind her. I turned my gaze to Coypu; uglier but safer.

"Then that is the one we must try," I told him.

"I thought you might say that. I have the parallelilizer screen projected outside this laboratory building. It is one hundred meters in diameter. I suggest you get a spacer with a smaller diameter and I will instruct you from there on."

"Great idea. A Lancer scoutship will just do the job."

I exited with my loyal crew right after me. I signed for the scoutship and did all the preflight checks with Angelina's assistance. Incuba stayed out of the control room, which made life easier to live.

"I've always wanted to see another universe," I said brightly.

"Shut up and fly this thing."

I sighed and got Coypu on the radio.

"Fly forty-six degrees from your present position," he said. *"You will see a circular ring of lights."*

"Got it."

"Then go through it. And I suggest you make a careful navigation fix on the other side and drop a radio beacon as well."

"Very helpful of you. We would like to get back someday."

The spacer slipped through the ring, which vanished behind us. In the rear scopes I could see a disc of blackness occulting the stars.

"Position recorded, beacon launched," Angelina said.

"You are wonderful. I note from the recordings that there is a nice G2 star over there about fifty light years away. And the radio tells me that it was emitting radio signals some fifty years ago. Shall we go look?"

"Yes. And that's all you will be looking at!"

"My love!" I took her hands in mine. "I have eyes only for you." Then I saw that she was smiling, then laughing and we clinched a bit. "You have been leading me on?" I accused.

"A little bit. I thought it would be fun to go on this trip and it seemed a good reason. Also I will flay you with broken glass if you go anywhere near that Morality Corps chicken."

"No fear. I am too busy saving the galaxy once again."

When we came out of warpdrive Incuba joined us at the controls.

"There are two inhabited planets about that sun?" she asked.

"That is what the instruments and the radio tell us. We are taking a look-see at the nearest."

It was a quick jump by warpdrive and then we were dropping down into the atmosphere. Blue sky, white clouds, a very pleasant place. The radio was blaring out very sinister music and occasional bursts of some incomprehensible language. None of us felt like talking. What, or who, inhabited this planet was of utmost importance. Lower and lower until the landscape was clear below us.

"Houses," Angelina said, sounding very unhappy. "And plowed fields. Looks very much like home . . ."

"No, it doesn't," I shouted, turning up the magnification.

"Beautiful!" Angelina sighed, and it was. At least at this moment. Something with far too many legs was pulling a plow. Steering the plow was a very repulsive alien who would have been right at home with our present enemies.

"An alien universe!" I laughed as I spoke. "They can come here and make friends and live happily ever after. Let's go back with the good news."

"Let us investigate the other planet," Incuba said quietly. "And as many more as we have to determine if humans exist here as well."

Angelina gave her a cold look and I sighed.

"Sure. That's what we must do. Look around and make sure it is all creepies. Of course it will be."

Old big mouth. We zipped over to the second inhabited planet and looked down upon mills and mines, cities and countryside. Inhabited by the most human-looking humans I have ever seen.

"Maybe they are alien inside," I said, grasping at a last straw.

"Should we cut one open and find out?" Angelina asked seriously.

"The cutting open of other creatures, human or alien, is forbidden by the Morality Corps . . ."

Incuba's words were cut off by a blast of static from the radio and shouted words in a strange language. At the same moment a number of readouts flickered and I looked at the viewscreen. And drew back.

"We have company," I said. "Shall we leave?"

"I wouldn't do anything in a hurry," Angelina cozened.

For outside, very close indeed, was a very nasty black warship. Some of the guns had gaping muzzles big enough to drive our small ship into. And I'm sure that it was not by chance that they were pointing at us. I reached for the thrust controls just as I felt a number of strong tractor beams latch onto our ship.

"I think I will flit over and talk to them," I said, rising and going to the suit locker. "Just watch the shop until I get back."

"I'm going with you," Angelina said firmly.

"Not this time, light of my life. And that is a command. If I don't get back try and get a report through about what we have seen."

With this noble exit line I exited, suited up and floated over to the dreadnought where a port obligingly opened for me. I walked in, head up, and was cheered a bit to see that the reception party were all human. Hard-eyed types in tight black uniforms.

"Krzty picklin stimfrx!" the one with the most gold bullion snapped at me.

"I'm sure it's a great language, but I don't speak it."

He cocked an ear and listened—then issued a sharp order. Men ran and returned with a metal box, wires, plugs and a nasty-looking helmet. I shied away from the thing, but efficient-looking weapons were ground into my ribs and I desisted. It was clapped over my head, adjustments were made, then the officer spoke again.

"Can you understand me now, worm of an intruder?" he asked.

"I certainly can and there is no need for such language. We have come a long way and I don't need any insults from you."

His lips peeled back from his teeth at that and I thought he was going to sink them into my throat. The others present gasped with shock.

"Do you know who I am!" he shouted.

"No, nor do I care. Because you don't know who I am. You have the pleasure of being in the presence of the first ambassador from a parallel universe. So you might say hello."

"He is telling the truth," a technician said, watching his flickering needles.

"Well, that's different," the officer said. Calming instantly. "You wouldn't be expected to know the quarantine restrictions. My name is Kangg. Come have a drink and tell me what you are doing here."

The booze was not bad and they were all fascinated by my story. Before I had finished they sent for the ladies and we all clinked glasses.

"Well, good luck on your quest," Kangg said, raising his glass. "I don't envy you your job. But as you can see we have our alien problem licked and the last thing we need is an invasion. Our war ended about a thousand years ago and was a close-run thing. We blew up all the alien spaceships and made sure the creepos stay now on planets of their own. They are ready to go for our throats again at any time, so we keep an eye on them with patrols like mine."

"We shall return home and I shall report it would be immoral to send the fleet here," Incuba said.

"We can lend you a few battleships," Kangg offered. "But we are really spread kind of thin."

"I'll report your offer, and thanks," I said. "But I'm afraid we need a more drastic solution. Now we have to get back because we will need an answer soon, or else."

"Hope you lick them. Those greenies can be very mean."

It was with utmost gloom that we returned to our ship and set course for the beacon. The parallel-world booze must have been working in my brain, or desperation goosing it into top gear, because suddenly I had a most interesting thought.

"I have it!" I shouted with uncontrolled joy. "The answer to our problems at last." We popped through the screen and I made a mad landing at the nearest airlock. "Come with me and hear what it is!"

I ran, with the girls right behind me, bursting into the meeting room just as the staff chiefs were gathering in answer to my emergency call.

"Then we can send them the aliens?" Inskipp asked.

"No way. They have alien problems of their own."

"Then what do we do?" a senile admiral moaned. "Six parallel galaxies and all of them with human beings. Where do we send the aliens?"

"To none of them," I said. "We send them somewhere else instead. I checked with Coypu and he says it is possible and he is muttering over the equations now."

"Where? Tell us!" Inskipp ordered.

"Why, we use time travel. We send them through time."

"Into the past?" He was puzzled.

"No, that wouldn't work. They would just be hanging around waiting for the human race to develop so they could wipe us out. So the past is no good. We send them into the future."

"You're mad, diGriz. What does that accomplish?"

"Look, we send them a hundred years into the future. And while they are en route we have all the best scientific minds of the galaxy working on ways to knock them off. We have a hundred years to do it in. We develop something and, a hundred years from now, our people are waiting for them when they appear and they take care of the menace once and for all."

"Wonderful!" Angelina said. "My husband is a genius. Set up the machine and send them into the future."

"IT IS FORBIDDEN," a deep voice said from above.

TWENTY

The shocked silence that followed this unexpected announcement continued for a heartbeat or two, then was interrupted drastically when Inskipp whipped out his gun and began shooting holes in the ceiling.

"Secret meeting! Top security! Why don't we go on TV with this session—it would be more private!"

He foamed as he spoke and shrugged off the aged admirals who tried to stop him. I vaulted the table and disarmed him, numbing him a bit in the process so he dropped, glassy-eyed, into his chair where he muttered to himself.

"Who said that?" I called out.

"I did," a man said, appearing suddenly in midair, accompanied by a sharp popping sound. He dropped the short distance to the table, then jumped neatly to the floor.

"It beith I who spake, noble sirs. I hite Ga Binetto."

He was something interesting to look at, dressed in baggy velvet clothes with high boots, a big hat with a curly feather, curly mustachios too which he twirled with his free hand. The other hand rested on the pommel of his sword. Since Inskipp was still muttering I would have to talk to him.

"We don't care how tall you are—what's your name?"

"Name? Namen—verily. I am named Ga Binetto."

"What gives you the right to come barging into a secret meeting like this?"

"Forsooth, there be no secrets hidden from ye Temporal Constabulary."

"The Time Police?" This was something new. "Time travelers from the past?" This was beginning to confuse even me.

"Ods bodkins, varlet, nay! Why thinkest thou that?"

"I thinkest that because that outfit and language haven't been around for maybe thirty-two thousand years."

He flashed me a dirty look and made some quick adjustments on some knobs on the pommel of his sword.

"Don't be so damn superior," Ga Binetto snapped. "You try hopping from time to time and learning all the disgusting languages and dialects. Then you wouldn't be so quick to . . ."

"Can we get back to business," I broke in. "You're the Time Police, but not from the past. So—let me guess—the future maybe? Just nod your head, that's right. So that's straight. Now tell us why we can't shoot those aliens through a couple of hundred years of time?"

"Because it is forbidden."

"You said that before. Now, how about some reasons."

"I don't have to give you any." He leered coldly. "We could have sent an H-bomb through instead of me, so how about shutting up and listening."

"He is correct," one of the senile admirals quavered. "Welcome to our time, illustrious time traveler. Give us your instructions, if you please."

"That's more like it. Respect where respect is due, if you don't mind. All you are permitted to know is that it is the job of the Time Police to police time. We see to it that paradoxes do not occur, that major misuses of time travel, such as your proposed plan, do not happen. The very fabric of time and probability would be strained by the event should it occur. It is forbidden."

There was a gloomy silence following this news, during which time I thought furiously.

"Tell me, Ga Binetto," I said. "Are you human or an alien in disguise?"

"I'm as human as you," he said angrily. "Maybe even more so."

"That's good. Then if you are a human from the future the aliens never wiped out all the human beings in the galaxy as they plan. Right?"

"Then how do we win the war?"

"The war is won by . . ." He clamped his mouth shut and turned bright red. "That information is time-classified and I cannot tell you. Figure it out for yourself."

"Don't palm us off with that chromo-crap," Inskipp growled, deep in his throat, recovered at last. "You say stop the only plan that can save the human race. Sure I say, we'll stop it—if you tell us what else we can do. Or we go ahead as planned."

"It is forbidden to tell."

"Can't you at least hint?" I suggested.

He thought about that for a moment, then smiled. I did not like the look of that smile. "The solution should be obvious to one of your intelligence, diGriz. It's all in the mind."

He hopped into the air, clicked his heels together—and disappeared.

"What did he mean by that?" Inskipp said, scowling with concentration.

What did he mean? It was a clue directed at me so I should be able to solve the riddle. The first part was there to misdirect me I was sure, the bit about my intelligence. *It's all in the mind.* My mind? Whose mind? Was it an idea we had not thought of before? Or was he really talking about minds? I had no idea.

Incuba was looking dreamily into space, thinking deep moral thoughts no doubt. I was beginning to think she was pretty dumb. But not Angelina. That lovely brow was furrowed with thought, for her mind was as highpowered as her body. She narrowed her eyes, concentrating—then suddenly widened them. Then smiled. When she caught me looking at her the smile broadened, and she winked. I raised my eyebrows, in an unspoken question and she nodded back, ever so slightly.

If I were reading the signs correctly all of this nonverbal communication indicated that she had solved the riddle. Having seen recently what real male chauvinist swine were, I was beginning to abandon my claim to that role. If Angelina had the answer I would humbly and with gratitude accept it from her. I leaned closer.

"If you know—tell us," I said. "Credit where credit is due."

"You are maturing as the years pass, aren't you, darling!" She blew me a quick kiss, then raised her voice. "Gentlemen. The answer is obvious."

"Well, not to me," Inskipp said.

"It's all in the mind, that's what he said. Which can mean mind control . . ."

"The gray men!" I shouted. "The Kekkonshiki brain kinkers!"

"I still don't see . . ."

"Because you can see only a physical battle, Inskipp old warrior," I said. "What that time traveling twit was hinting at was an end to the war completely."

"How?"

"By getting the aliens to change their minds. By having them learn to love human beings so they can turn their industrial might to war reparations and make this universe a model for all the others. And who are the master mind changers? None but the Kekkonshiki. They told me that their psychcontrol techniques work on all races. Let's put them to the test."

"And how do you think they will do that?" an admiral asked.

"The details will be worked out later," I said, meaning I hadn't the slightest idea at this time. "Order up a battle cruiser and see that there are plenty of space marines aboard. I am off at once to arrange the salvation of the galaxy."

"I am not sure about that," Incuba said. "There is a question of morality in mind manipulation . . ." Her words died away and she slumped to the floor.

"Poor thing, she's fainted," Angelina said. "All the stress, you know. I'll take her to her quarters."

Fainted indeed! I had seen my wife in action before. As she spirited the unconscious girl from the room I moved fast, taking advantage of the time she had bought me.

"The battle cruiser! Order it to the spacelock now for I am going to board her."

"Correct," Inskipp said. "It's on its way." He was aware of the byplay too and just as eager as I was to get the project launched while the Morality Corps observer was accidentally indisposed.

We made a fast and silent trip. For security measures I imposed a radio blackout from repeater stations and told the psiman to accept no messages directed at us. So when the frigid world of Kekkonshiki appeared on the screens ahead I still had not been ordered back. And, after giving the subject a good deal of concentration, I knew what had to be done.

"Break radio blackout and contact the landing party," I ordered.

"They're on now," the operator said. "But they haven't landed. Their ship is still in orbit."

"What's happened?"

"Here's the commander, sir."

An officer with a bandaged head appeared on the screen. He saluted when he saw all the gold braid I was wearing.

"They insist on fighting," he said. "My orders were to pacify the planet, not blow it up. So when all attempts at communication failed I withdrew. After neutralizing their spacers."

"They know they can't win."

"You know that and I know that. Now try telling it to those madmen."

It should have been expected. The fatalistic Kekkon-shiki would much prefer to die than surrender. In fact surrender was probably a word that they did not know, a concept alien to their Moral Philosophy of survival. Yet we needed their help. There was only one person on the planet—hopefully still alive—who could possibly arrange that.

"Stay in orbit, Commander, and await instructions. This ship will join you after I have made contact on the planet. You'll hear from me when it is time to land."

Within an hour I had issued all the orders, gathered what equipment I would need, and was floating down in a spacesuit toward the white planet below. The gravchute slowed my drop and the infrared scope let me see clearly through the driving snow. I steered for a familiar building and dropped, not too lightly, onto a roof where I had been before. It was all very cold and very depressing because I had hoped I had seen the last of this particular world.

I suppose I could have landed on the ground and gone in through the front door, taken a squad of marines too to help me shoot up any opposition. But that was not what I wanted. A quiet contact with Hanasu first, before anyone knew I was back. The fact that it was well after dark had convinced me that retracing my old route might be the best way. I pried open the trapdoor and, after much wriggling and puffing, managed to get myself and the spacesuit through the opening and into the building. First step accomplished. Then I took off the cumbersome garment, unlocked the door for what I hoped was the last time, and walked silently down the corridor.

"You are the enemy, you must be killed," a small boy said in a toneless voice as he hurled himself at me. I stepped aside so he stumbled and fell, leaving me the perfect target. The needle from my gun easily penetrated the seat of his trousers and he sighed and relaxed. I tucked him under my arm and went on as quietly as I could.

By the time I pushed open Hanasu's office door I was carrying four of them altogether and beginning to stagger. He looked up from behind the desk and, if he were capable of smiling, this is the time when he would have.

"It all worked as you planned," he said. "The message was received. You escaped."

"I did, and now I'm back. With some small friends who are not happy to see me."

"They listen to the radio broadcasts from Kome and they do not know what to believe. They are disturbed."

"Well, these ones are quiet enough now. Let me make them comfortable on your floor."

"I will use the axion feed. They will remember nothing."

"Not this time. They'll sleep long enough not to bother us. Now tell me—what has happened since I left."

"Confusion. It is written nowhere in our Moral Philosophy what to do at this sort of time. Therefore when Kome issued his orders to fight or die he was obeyed. Everyone can understand that. There was no way I could combat him by myself, so I have done nothing. I have waited."

"Very wise. But now that I am here there is something very important that you can do."

"What is that?"

"Convince your people here that they must take up alien disguise again and go back and control the aliens."

"I do not understand. You wish them to encourage the war again?"

"No. Quite the opposite. I want them to stop it."

"You must explain. This is beyond me."

"Let me ask you a question first. Could the synaptic generators be used on the aliens? To convince them that human beings are really very nice after all. We do have damp eyeballs and sweat a lot. Fingers aren't too different from tentacles when you think about it. Could this be done?"

"Very easily. You must understand that the aliens come from primitive cultures and are easily led. When we began infiltrating them to organize the invasion we were faced with indifference at first. To overcome this the leaders were treated and taught to hate humans.

Then, through propaganda, they convinced the rest of the populations. It took a long time, but that is the way it was done."

"Can the indoctrination process be reversed?"

"I would think so. But how can you convince my people to do a thing like this?"

"That is the big question I was coming to." I stood and paced the room, marshaling my thoughts, stepping over the snoring bodies of the boys. "What is to be done must be done through the teachings of Moral Philosophy as you practice it here. I was wrong, angry, when I told you that this culture must be destroyed. It should not be. It is a vital one, an important one that contains elements that should benefit all of mankind. It was just misapplied when it left the surface of this planet. Is there anything inherent in Moral Philosophy, MP, that says you must be galaxy conquerors?"

"No. We learned to hate those who abandoned us on this world because we must always believe that they will never come back to save us. We must save ourselves. Survival is the beginning and the end. Anything that goes against that is wrong."

"Then Kome and his talk of racial suicide is wrong!"

For a Kekkonshiki, Hanasu looked almost startled. "Of course! His preachings go against the law. All must be told."

"They will be. But that is point one. Now think about the laws of MP again. You survive. You are superior to the rest of mankind. You hate the ones who abandoned you long ago. But the people alive today don't even know about that abandonment, nor are they responsible for it. Therefore it is not necessary to hate them. Better than that, since the Kekkonshiki are superior to all other people, you are morally responsible to help them survive if they are threatened. How does that fit the MP rules?"

Hanasu was wide-eyed and rigid, his mind in a turmoil as he considered these unusual ideas. Nodding his head.

"It is just as you say. It is a novel thing to apply Moral Philosophy to a new situation. It has never been done before. There were no new situations. There are now. We have been wrong and I see now how we have been wrong. We simply reacted to other human beings. *We were emotional.* We violated the basic tenets of Moral Philosophy. When I explain all will understand. We will save the human race." He turned to me and clasped my hand. "You have saved us from ourselves, my friend. We have broken the tenets by what we have done. Now we will make them right. I will go forth and speak."

"Let's set it up. We must be sure that Kome doesn't shoot first and debate later. If we keep him quiet do you think that you can convince the troops?"

"There is no doubt. None will dare disagree with what I say for I will explain the law as it is written, as it is taught, as they have learned since they were small boys like the ones here."

As though right on cue some of these same small boys burst the door open. There were a lot of them there, filling the doorway, all heavily armed. Led by one of their teachers who pointed the gun directly at me.

"Put down your weapon," he ordered. "I will shoot and kill if you do not."

TWENTY-ONE

Of course my gun was pointing at the pack; my reflexes are still in good shape. I had drawn and crouched automatically as the door had crunched. Now I rose slowly and let the gun drop to my side. I was seriously outgunned, by deadly weapons held by nervous boys.

"Don't shoot, you've got me cold!" I called out.

"What is the meaning of this?" Hanasu asked, standing and walking toward the door. "Lower those weapons. This is an order."

The boys obeyed instantly—they knew who the headmaster was—but the teacher wavered. "Kome has said . . ."

"Kome is not here. Kome is wrong. I order you for the last time to put that weapon down." The teacher hesitated for an instant too long and Hanasu turned to me. "Shoot him," he ordered.

Of course I did, and he thudded to the floor. With a sleep needle of course, though the boys did not have to know that. And I doubted if Hanasu cared. He was not used to his orders being disobeyed. "Hand me that gun," he ordered the nearest boy. "And call an assembly of the entire school at once."

They handed over the guns and instantly left. I dragged in the teacher's body and laid it next to his pupils. Hanasu closed the door, deep in thought.

"Here is what we will do," he finally said. "I will explain the differences to everyone in terms of Moral Philosophy. They have been troubled with internal conflicts over the application and this problem will now be resolved. After they have understood we will march on the spaceport. Kome and his activists are there. I will explain again and they will join us. Then you will call your ship down and we will proceed to the second part of the program."

"That all sounds very good. But what if they don't agree with you?"

"They will have to. Because it is not me they are agreeing with but the text of Moral Philosophy as it is written. Once they understand it will not be a matter of choice or agreement but of obedience."

He sounded very sure of himself so I crossed my fingers behind his back and hoped that he was right.

"Maybe I should come with you. In case of trouble?"

"You will wait here until you are summoned."

Hanasu exited on that line and I could do nothing other than let him go. The row of unconscious figures depressed me, so I unlimbered my radio and contacted my ships; to put them into the picture. They would stand by, in orbit above the spaceport, and await further orders. I broke the connection when there was a knock on the door.

"Come with me," a stern-faced little boy ordered. I obeyed. Hanasu was waiting by the open front door of the school while boys and teachers streamed by him on both sides.

"We go to the spaceport," he said. "We will reach it at dawn."

"No problems?"

"Of course not. I could tell that they were relieved to have this conflict over interpretation of the rulings of Moral Philosophy made clear to them. My people are strong, but they get their strength from obedience. Now they are stronger still."

Hanasu drove the only car in the procession and I was glad to travel with him. The rest of the staff and the students slogged along on skis. Uncomplainingly, despite the fact they had all been sound asleep less than an hour before. There is a lot to be said for discipline. There is nothing to be said for the comfort of Kekkonshiki groundcars. Though this trip was a little smoother than the first one, since Hanasu drove slower so the skiers could keep up. Dawn was lighting up the first snowstorm of the morning as we reached the spaceport entrance. Two guards emerged from the shack and looked stolidly at the car and following skiers as though this happened every day.

"Tell Kome I am here to see him," Hanasu ordered.

"None are permitted in. Kome has ordered. All enemy are to be killed. That is an enemy in your car. Kill him."

Hanasu's voice was cold as the grave, although it rang with authority.

"The Fourteenth Rule of Obedience states you will obey the orders of one of the Ten. I have given you an order. There is no rule that there are enemies to be killed. Stand aside."

A trace of emotion almost touched the guard's face, then was gone. He stepped back. "Proceed," he said. "Kome will be informed."

In line now, our juvenile and senile invading force swept across the spaceport toward the administration buildings. We passed antiaircraft implacements, but the men manning them only looked on and made no attempt to stop us. It was gray, chill dawn now, with sudden snow flurries blasting by. Our car stopped in front of the entrance to administration and Hanasu had just climbed, creaking, down when the door opened. I stayed in the car and tried to look invisible. Kome and a dozen followers emerged, all carrying guns.

It must have been the cold that was chilling my brain because I realized, for the first time, that I was the only one in our party who was armed.

"Go back to your school, Hanasu. You are not wanted here," Kome shouted, getting in the first word. Hanasu ignored him, walking forward until he was face to face with the other man. When he spoke he spoke loudly so all could hear.

"I tell you all to put your guns away for what you are doing is against the rule of Moral Philosophy. By that rule we must lead the weak races. By that rule we must not commit suicide by fighting all the other races who outnumber us millions to one. If we fight them as we are doing now we will all be killed. Is this what the Thousand taught us? You must . . ."

"You must get out of here," Kome called out. "It is you who break the rule. Go or be killed." He raised his gun and pointed it. I slipped out of the door of the car.

"I wouldn't do that if I were you," I said, my own gun pointing.

"You bring an alien here!" Kome's voice was loud, almost angry. "He will be killed, you will be killed . . ."

His voice broke off and there was a loud crack as Hanasu stepped forward and slapped him hard across the face.

"You are proscribed," Hanasu said, and there was a gasp of indrawn breath from all the watchers. "You have disobeyed. You are ended."

"Ended? Not me, you!" Kome cracked, his voice roared with rage, whipping up his gun.

I dived to the side, trying for a shot, but Hanasu was in the way. There was the crackling roar of gunfire.

Yet Hanasu still stood there. Unmoving as Kome's ragged body fell to the ground. All of his followers had fired at him at the same time. The rule of Kekkonshiki Moral Philosophy had destroyed him. Calm and undisturbed, Hanasu turned to all those present and explained his newly discovered interpretation of the Law. They tried not to show expression, but it was obvious that they were relieved. There was solidity in their lives again, structure and order. Kome's huddled body was the only evidence that there had ever been a schism and, from the way they stood, they obviously did not see it nor want to look at it. Order had returned.

"You can come down now," I ordered into my radio.

"Negative. Priority override orders."

"Negative!" I shouted into the microphone. "What are you talking about. Get those crates down here instantly or I'll fry your commander and eat him for lunch."

"Negative. Order issuing vessel on way ETA three minutes."

The connection was broken and I could only stare, popeyed, at the radio. What development was this? More and more men were coming up and listening to Hanasu. The situation was well in hand, a solution possible—and I got more troubles. A slim scoutship dropped down through the snowstorms and I was at the port when it swung open. Fire in my eye and my fingers twitching millimeters from my gunbutt. A familiar and loathsome form stepped out.

"You!" I cried.

"Yes, it is I. And just in time to prevent a miscarriage of moral justice."

It was Jay Hovah, boss of the Morality Corps. And I had more than a strong suspicion why he was here.

"You're not needed here," I said. "Nor are you dressed for the weather. I suggest you get back inside."

"Morality comes first," he shivered, for no one had told him about the climate and he was wearing just his usual bathrobe outfit.

"I tried talking to him, but he would not listen," an even more familiar voice said, and Angelina emerged from behind him.

"Darling!" I called out and we had a quick embrace then drew away as Jay Hovah's voice came between us.

"It is my understanding that your mission here is to convince these people to use psychcontrol techniques on the aliens so we can win the war. These techniques are immoral and will not be used."

"Who is this who comes here?" Hanasu asked in his coldest voice.

"His name is Jay," I said. "In charge of our Morality Corps. He makes sure that we don't do things that violate our own moral codes."

Hanasu looked him up and down like some specimen of vermin, then turned away and faced me. "I have seen him," he said. "You may now take him away. Have your ships land so the operation against the aliens can begin."

"I don't think you heard me," Jay Hovah said through chattering teeth. "This operation is forbidden. It is immoral."

Hanasu turned slowly to face him and impaled him with an arctic stare. "You do not talk to me of immorality. I am a Leader in Moral Philosophy and I interpret the Law. What we did to the aliens to start this war was a mistake. We will now utilize the same techniques to stop it."

"No! Two wrongs do not make a right. It is forbidden."

"You cannot stop us, for you have no authority here. You can only order us killed to stop us. If we are not killed we will do what must be done as ordered by our own moral code."

"You will be stopped . . ."

"Only by death. If you cannot order us killed remove yourself and your interference."

Hanasu turned his back and walked away. Jay moved his jaw a few times, but had trouble talking. He was also turning blue. I waved two of the schoolboys over.

"Here, lads. Help this poor old man back into his ship so he can warm up and consider the old philosophical problem of an irresistible force meeting an immovable object."

Jay tried to protest, but they gave him a firm clutch and frogmarched him back aboard.

"What happens now?" Angelina asked.

"The Kekkonshiki are unleashed and go out and try to win the war. There is no way that the Morality Corps can find justification for killing them in order to stop them from saving us. I think that will be a little too much hair-splitting even for Jay and Incuba. He can maybe order us not to give aid to the Kekkonshiki, but will probably have a hard time justifying even that."

"I'm sure that you are right. Then what is next?"

"Next? Why, saving the galaxy, of course. Again."

"That's my ever-modest husband," she said, but tempered her admonitory words by kissing me soundly.

TWENTY-TWO

"That really looks impressive, don't you think?" I asked.

"I think it looks disgusting," Angelina said, wrinkling her nose. "Not only that, they stink."

"An improvement over the first model. Remember, where we are going anything bad must be good."

In a way Angelina was right. It did look disgusting. Which was good, very good. We stood at the front of the main cabin of the spaceliner we had commandeered for this job. Before us stretched row after row of heavy chairs, almost five hundred in all. And in each chair there crouched, or flopped, or oozed, a singularly repulsive alien. Something to gladden the eyestalks of the enemy I was sure, for all of these had been patterned after my first alien disguise. More of the same race, the Geshtunken. What would not have gladdened the multiple hearts and plasma pumps of the enemy, if they had known, was the fact that each of these aliens held a solemn-faced Kekkonshiki. While built into each thrashing tail was a high-powered synaptic generator. Our crusade for peace had begun.

Not that organizing it had been easy. The Morality Corps was still resolutely set against our brain-twisting the enemy. But their authority worked through planetary governments and the heads of staff. For once I blessed the complex tangle of bureaucratic tanglement. While orders were issued and routed a few of us in the Special Corps launched a rush program to circumvent the orders before we received them. Key technicians were whisked away and their destination lost in the files. A protesting Prof Coypu was ripped from his midnight bed and found himself in deep space before he had put his socks on. A certain highly automated manufacturing planet had been co-opted by our agents and the Kekkonshiki volunteers were space-lifted there. While the alien disguises were being fabricated, Hanasu headed the programming team of psychcontrol technicians. We had barely succeeded in time, finally blasting off short hours ahead of the battleship that Morality Corps had dispatched to stop us. In the end this aided instead of hurting since we zipped up to the alien fleet with the battleship belting along after us. A few barrages from the space-whales had it turning tail.

"We're within communication distance now," I announced. "Are you ready for your work, Kekkonshiki volunteers?"

"We are ready," came the loud but unemotional response.

"Good luck, then. On suits, my crew."

I climbed into my alien outfit and Angelina got into hers. James was in one robot disguise, Bolivar in the other. They waved, then clanged the tops shut. I zipped my neck and turned on the communicator.

"My darling Sleepery Jeem returned from the grave!" a repulsive thing with claws and tentacles rattled and gurgled at me from the screen.

"I do not know you, ugly sir," I simpered. "But you must have made the acquaintance of my twin. I am her sister, Sleepery Bolivar." I actuated the trigger that released a large and oily tear that trickled down my lengthened eyelashes and splashed to the deck. "Back on Geshtunken we heard of her noble death. We have come for vengeance!"

"Welcome, welcome," the thing gurgled and writhed.

"I am Sess-Pula, the new commander of all the forces. Join me at once and we will have great stinking banquet!"

I did as ordered, joining our ships and rolling to his rotten welcome with Angelina at my side. I had to sidestep neatly to avoid Sess's wet embrace and he squashed to the deck instead.

"Meet Ann-Geel, my chief of staff. These little robots bring gifts of food and drink which we will now consume."

The party rolled into high gear at once, and more and more of the ship's officers came to join us until I wondered who was flying the thing. Probably no one. "How goes the war?" I asked.

"Terrible!" Sess moaned, draining a flagon, of something green and bubbly. "Oh, we have the alien crunchies on the run all right, but they won't stop and fight. Morale runs low since all of our soldiers are fed up with war and want only to return to the sticky embraces of their loved things. But the war must go on. I think."

"Help is on the way," I cried, slapping him on the back, then wiping off my hand on the rug. "My ship is filled with bloodthirsty volunteers all lusting for war and victory and vengeance. In addition to being great fighters and having good senses of smell, my troops are great navigators and fire control officers, watch-keeping officers and cooks."

"By Slime-Gog we can use them!" Sess gurgled aloud. "Do you have many troops with you?"

"Well," I said coyly. "We might just have enough to spare one for each of your battleships, and each battleship can lead a fleet, and if the officers of the fleet want advice or morale boosting they are welcome to talk to my people who work night and day and are sexy to boot."

"We are saved!" he screamed.

Or lost, I thought to myself, smiling toothily at the disgusting revelry on all sides. I wondered how long it would take for my brainscrambling saboteurs to get the job done.

Not long, not long at all. Since the aliens had had to be convinced to go to war in the first place, were fed up in the second place, they were ripe for subversion in the third place. The rot spread and it was only a few days later that Sess-Pula slithered up to me in the navigation room where I was making sure, by rotten navigation, that we didn't catch up with the fleeing human fleet. He looked gloomily at the screen with a half dozen bloodshot eyestalks.

"Not sleeping too well lately?" I asked, flicking one of his rudy orbs with a claw. He sucked it back in unhappily.

"You can say that again, bold Woleevar. It is all too depressing, the fleet seems to be getting away, back in my home hive last year's crop of virgins will be approaching estrous. I keep asking myself what I am doing here."

"What are you doing here?"

"I don't know. My heart has gone out of this war."

"Funny. I was thinking the same thing last night. Have you noticed that the aliens really aren't too crunchy? They have damp eyes and nasty-looking wet red things in their mouths."

"You're right!" he slobbered. "I never thought of that before. What can we possibly do?"

"Well . . ." I said, and for all apparent purposes that was that. Ten hours later, after a lot of radioing back and forth among the ships, the mightiest fighting armada the galaxy had ever seen was cutting a great arc in space. Turning, reversing, going back to the creepy places from whence they had come.

In the drunken party that evening that celebrated the victorious end of the war—they had rationalized it that way with some help—I and Angelina clutched claws and looked around at the disgusting sights on all sides.

"They are really sort of sweet when you get used to them," she said.

"I wouldn't go quite as far as to say that. But they are rather harmless once they abandon all the war plans."

"Rich, too," the James robot said, pouring something nasty into my glass.

"We have been doing a little investigating," Bolivar said, rolling up on the other side. "In their various operations they have captured ships and planets and satellites. They emptied all the bank vaults since they knew that we valued their contents, though they didn't know why. They do not have money as we have it."

"I know," I said. "They have the Eckh Unit, which is best left undescribed."

"Right, Dad," James said. "So when they raided all the treasuries they sent the stuff here to the command battleship, hoping something would figure out what to do with it. What they did do with it was to store it all in one of the holds."

"Let me guess," Angelina said. "The hold is now empty?"

"You're always right, Mom. And the transport ship is sort of full."

"We'll have to return the loot to the sources from whence it came," I said, and was pleased at the two shocked robotic looks and one alien stare of despair.

"Jim . . . !" Angelina gasped.

"Do not worry. I have all my senses. I mean we'll have to return the alien loot that we found . . ."

". . . but we didn't recover very much." She finished the sentence for me.

Something heavy, greenish-brown, tentacled and clawed, squashed down noisily next to me.

"To victory!" Sess-Pula shouted. "We must drink to victory! Silence, everyone, silence, while the pulchritudinous Sleepery proposes a toast."

"I shall!" I shouted, jumping to my feet. Aware of the sudden silence and the fact that every eyepad, eyestalk, optic tentacle, not to mention six human eyeballs, was fixed upon me.

"A toast," I called out, raising my glass on high so enthusiastically that some of the drink slopped out and burned a hole in the carpet.

"A toast to all the creatures that live in our universe, large and small, solid and sloppy. May peace and love be their lot forever more. Here's to life, liberty—and the opposite sex!"

And thus we rushed down the light years toward a far, far better future.

I hope.

ABOUT THE AUTHOR

HARRY HARRISON is one of our most prolific and success-
ful science fiction writers. His *Stainless Steel Rat* books
are as well known as they are humorous. His other
books include: *Deathworld*, *Deathworld 2*, and *Make
Room, Make Room*, his anti-utopian novel on which the
movie *Soylent Green* was based. Mr. Harrison worked as
a commercial artist, art director and editor before settling
on a career as a freelance writer. He was born in Connec-
ticut, has made his home in various European countries
over the years and now lives in Ireland. He is a past pres-
ident of the World Science Fiction Writers' Association
and has received numerous awards and honors.